The Sanctity of Hate

Books by Priscilla Royal

Wine of Violence
Tyrant of the Mind
Sorrow Without End
Justice for the Damned
Forsaken Soul
Chambers of Death
Valley of Dry Bones
A Killing Season
The Sanctity of Hate

The Sanctity of Hate

A Medieval Mystery

Priscilla Royal

Poisoned Pen Press

Poisoned Pen Press
6962 E. First Ave., Ste. 103
Scottsdale, AZ 85251
www.poisonedpenpress.com
info@poisonedpenpress.com

Printed in the United States of America

To Dianne Levy with gratitude and love.
Tyndal Priory and its inhabitants would be lost
without your web design artistry.

Acknowledgments

Maggie Anton; Christine and Peter Goodhugh; Earl Flewellen (E. G. Flewellen's Bee Farm of Port Costa, California); and Samuel Spurrier (Master of Berthaville); Ed Kaufman; Henie Lentz; Dianne Levy; Sharon Kay Penman; Barbara Peters (Poisoned Pen Bookstore in Scottsdale, Arizona); Robert Rosenwald and all the staff of Poisoned Pen Press; Marianne and Sharon Silva; Lyn and Michael Speakman; the staff of the University Press Bookstore (Berkeley, California).

Chapter One

A fat sun sat on the earth's wide edge, weary of the long summer hours and yearning to surrender to the reluctant darkness.

For the midges, it was frenzy time. They swarmed low over the mill pond where sharp-winged swallows swooped to dine in the insect cloud. Nearer the rising ground, massive black flies slowly gathered. Thanks to the carnage of midges, the flies were left in peace, using their freedom to seek a rotted fish or drowned creature upon which to feast and lay their eggs in the safety of the muddy bank.

They were soon to be rewarded.

In the slow-growing shadows, the mill wheel at Tyndal Priory turned with a deep groan, the great paddles squealing to a brief halt, then juddering forward to drop glistening water into the pond below. There the water grew dull and flowed lazily into the uneven patches of deep shade along the banks edged with thick rushes.

Pushed by the gentle current, a dark object floated toward the rank greenery. Bumping against the dense vegetation, it twisted to the side and an arm rose out of the water. The gesture might have been a greeting or perhaps a plea for help.

Neither gesture was intended. As the body turned in the rippling water, a man's head emerged. His eyes, clouded with death, stared at the unseen sky. A deep gash exposed raw flesh inside his neck.

The flies quickly settled on the wound in such number that the cruel injury was covered by their churning blackness.

Thus does nature look after the defenseless dead.

Chapter Two

A cool breeze from the North Sea wafted through the open window and sweetened the audience chamber with the apple-honey scent of chamomile and a hint of overripe apricot from the fading, but still yellow woodland oxlips.

Prioress Eleanor was grateful for it. As she sat, straight-backed in her carved chair, she breathed deeply of the refreshing fragrance. Her pleasure would remain unspoken, but the brief respite from the summer heat sharpened her attention to the words of the pair before her.

Prior Andrew and her sub-prioress, Sister Ruth, were having a most unusual debate.

At stake was the admission of a young man who had begged entry to Tyndal Priory as a novice, a rare occurrence for this Fontevraudine priory on the remote East Anglian coast. In such matters, Prior Andrew was usually the cautious one. In contrast, Sister Ruth grew eager if the supplicant carried either wealth in his beseeching hands or exuded that sweet perfume of noble birth, a scent that invariably brought joy to her heart.

This morning's discussion presented an uncommon reversal.

"We know the family," the prior said. "Master Oseberne is a well-regarded baker in the village. There is no reason to suspect he will not honor his promise of a gold candlestick and a gift of bread for the hospital on one day each month." He frowned, an odd gesture of perturbation from this kind-hearted man.

Sister Ruth's glare was more in character. "The family is worthy enough for village folk. It is their son that I like not."

"He's a pious lad from all I've heard."

"I have lived in Tyndal longer than you, Prior. I remember when he was a wee boy and slipped into our grounds to throw rocks at our nuns on their way to prayer."

"And how old was this child?"

"Old enough to stand on two feet, be draped with a seamless garment to cover his nakedness, and find his way through the mill gate." Folding her arms, Sister Ruth settled into obstinacy.

Eleanor raised an eyebrow and turned to await her prior's response.

He shrugged.

Sister Ruth's eyes narrowed.

The prioress molded her expression into one of expectant benevolence, then gently tapped her staff of office on the ground to remind both that she was waiting for further elaboration of positions.

"We are bound to forgive and obliged to show charity." Prior Andrew studied Sister Ruth as if searching for signs of these virtues in her face. Quickly he looked away, sadness in his eyes as he failed to discover any trace. "Young Adelard is no longer a babe," he said with a gentle tone. "I think he has grown into a wiser youth who now longs to serve God."

"Is a gold candlestick payment enough for the scar left on the cheek of the nun he struck?"

Eleanor rarely felt kinship with this woman, who often opposed her, but that remark touched her heart.

"Two candlesticks, perhaps?" The moment the words escaped his lips, Andrew knew the comment was better left unspoken. It sounded like a mockery of Sister Ruth. His face flushed with regret.

Oblivious to any insult, the sub-prioress turned thoughtful and jabbed a finger against her thin lower lip. "His father could not pay for so many. Indeed, I wonder that he can afford the one. I remember when his roof leaked and only the poorest ate his gritty bread."

"Which, not long ago, would have been most of those living nearby." Andrew swept his hand around the room, suggesting inclusion of all lands belonging to both village and priory. "God has smiled on us in recent years. The baker and his family now live in a finer house, and he even sells his bread to Mistress Signy when her own stores at the inn run short. As more people travel to our priory, many in the village have prospered as have we who are in God's service."

"In no small measure because our hospital infirmarian, Sister Christina, has wrought many miracles with her prayers for the sick and dying." The sub-prioress' arrogant expression faded as she glanced uneasily at Eleanor. "Although many questioned the sanctity of our anchoress after she was first entombed, sinners now journey here from all over England to consult with her."

Since the sub-prioress had been one of those detractors, Eleanor greeted this subtle concession with a gracious nod. As for the efficacy of priory medical treatment, Eleanor never ignored Sister Christina's pleas to God, she being a woman surely bound for the name of *blessed*, if not *saint*. But Eleanor also knew that both the renown and prosperity of the hospital owed much to the more worldly healing skills of Sister Anne, apothecary and sub-infirmarian.

An olive-brown bird flew through the open window and over the heads of the trio. Landing on a nearby table, the small chiffchaff chirped with bright song as if eager to add his opinion.

Sister Ruth eyed the bird with suspicion.

Prior Andrew also glanced at the creature and without thinking ran his hand over his bald head. "Do you have cause to believe Adelard has not changed his ways since the last rock was thrown?"

"No." Her reply was hesitant, and she began to twitch.

Suspecting an attack of fleas, Eleanor restrained herself from offering one of her linen pouches of lavender as an antidote.

"He spends much time in prayer at the priory church. Brother John says that he begs answers on questions of scripture and faith."

"His father's prosperity is recent. Dare we conclude that he will always be able to provide the bread promised, even if he does present us with the promised candlestick? Men of such birth..." The sub-prioress sniffed.

"Surely your objection is not based solely on his low worldly rank," Andrew said with annoyance. "In the village, that means little. Other than the crowner, no one there is of noble birth."

Eleanor was also growing impatient. "The baker's offer of one candlestick is adequate to brighten any altar," she said, "and his gift of bread to feed our sick honors charity. As for lasting affluence, we must never assume that prosperity shall continue beyond this moment, and that caution includes our priory. We would do well to recall the lesson of Job."

With a sharp twitter, the chiffchaff took wing, circled the room, and fled the chambers. Eleanor wondered if it had grown bored with the concerns of those God chose to rule the earth and all its beasts. Then she noticed a small white drop on the sub-prioress' shoulder, and amusement briefly pulled her thoughts down to a less celestial plane.

Sister Ruth's face was deepening to the color of a fine wine from the Aquitaine.

"Nor does our Order turn aside any with a true calling to serve God," Andrew said.

Eleanor nodded. "The mother house in Anjou serves as our model by taking not only the children of craftsmen but repentant prostitutes as well. All souls are equal in God's eyes."

"Surely we need not follow their practices in every respect!" Sister Ruth's forehead began to glisten, and the sour odor of fear wafted from her square body. "The abbey is large, and our small priory does not have the space or resources to imitate their singular benevolence."

Eleanor took mercy on the woman. "To our grief, you are correct. Even though our village is poor in magdalenes, we may at least follow the mother house's example and accept novices of lowlier parentage."

Andrew gestured with enthusiasm. "And we have done so already, much to the benefit of our priory and hospital. Sister Anne's father was a physician. Brother John was an apothecary when he lived in the world…"

The sub-prioress waved his observation aside. "The charity of our hospital is ultimately under the guidance of the infirmarian, Sister Christina, who is not only a woman of inestimable virtue but is also the daughter of…"

Eleanor thudded her staff on the floor. "We are drifting from the purpose of this discussion. The question before us is whether or not to admit Adelard, son of Oseberne the baker, as a novice to our priory."

The prior swatted at a fly. "I believe we should."

"I disagree." Sister Ruth sat upright with an implacable rigidity. Her thick body probably resembled the unyielding curtain wall of her noble brother's Norman fortress.

Shutting her eyes, the prioress knew she had lost patience. Her two subordinates had failed to compromise and seemed unwilling ever to do so. Could this meeting grow any more difficult?

When she heard a soft knock on the chamber door, Eleanor gratefully gave permission to enter.

As she stepped into the room, Gytha, the prioress' maid, looked uncommonly pale. "I beg pardon for the interruption, my lady."

Exuding rank displeasure at the intrusion, Sister Ruth eloquently turned her head away and muttered something incomprehensible.

"You surely have cause," Eleanor replied with especial gentleness. Her usually cheerful maid was uncommonly subdued.

Gytha bit her lip. "Brother Gwydo has found a man's body in the mill pond. He prays that you may come as soon as possible."

There was a collective gasp in the room.

"Send Brother Beorn to inform Crowner Ralf," the prioress replied as she rose from her chair and firmly gripped her staff of office. Then she gestured to her prior and sub-prioress. "We shall meet him at the site."

Although Eleanor knew no one could hear it, she could feel her heart pounding as if the Devil himself was beating a drum within her breast.

Chapter Three

Crowner Ralf heaved the corpse out of the water, dragged it to a wider part of the bank, and dropped it on the mud. Kneeling in the slimy muck, he rested his chin on his fist. "Not a pretty death," he said and stuck a finger into the neck wound to measure the depth. He looked up at the prioress standing near the edge of the bank. "That act took force and a long, sharp knife."

Eleanor bit her lip and nodded.

Grabbing a handful of tunic, he flipped the corpse over and pulled the man's black hair away from his neck. "There was a blow here as well." He pointed to the injury just under the man's ear.

The prioress stepped nearer the edge, as if considering whether to join the crowner in the mud, then knelt where she was and bent forward so she might better see the body. "Do you conclude that the head wound was suffered before his throat was slashed?"

"So I might. Why slit his throat, then strike him on the head? Unless, of course, the injury was suffered in a fall just after his throat was cut." He fingered the back of the man's head. "The bone is soft here. I'd say the blow might have cracked his skull, but I feel no loose fragments." He rocked back on his haunches and looked around. "The stream banks are higher where it flows through the forest." He gestured toward the village. "Had he fallen there, his head might have struck a large rock, but this is summer and the water level is low. He would not have fallen into the stream. Most likely, he was killed near the water and either fell or was pushed in."

"Why was he floating in our mill pond?" Eleanor considered the short distance between priory wall and the pond with apparent unease.

The turning mill wheel groaned loudly as if protesting innocence of the crime.

Ralf rose to his feet with a grunt. "There is no cause to suspect anything besides chance occurrence for the body to be here, my lady. The hands and face on the corpse have swollen. From my experience, I'd say the body has probably been in the water for a couple of days at least. Cuthbert is searching the stream bank outside this priory. It shouldn't take long for my sergeant to discover where the fight took place. This death is the king's problem."

"A fight?" Prior Andrew frowned as he pointed to the mutilated neck of the corpse. "You think that was the result of some petty disagreement?"

"A slashed throat suggests more than a minor quarrel between men with too much ale in their bellies," Eleanor said.

"I would agree," Ralf replied, "which may make solving this crime an easier matter."

"So you believe the corpse drifted downstream, into priory grounds, and went over the mill wheel with the cascading water?" She raised a hand to shade her eyes from the sun, then looked down at Ralf. "As you said, the water level in the stream is low. If this man died farther up the road to Norwich, wouldn't someone have seen the body as it floated past the village?"

"Unless he was killed at night. Then the body would have passed unnoticed, entered the pool above the mill where it may have sunk until the force of the water flowing over the wheel pulled it forward. You may be confident, my lady, that this death is under King Edward's jurisdiction."

Eleanor folded her arms as she considered this. Her expression suggested polite doubt.

"If I may, I would look upon the body, my lady." Sister Ruth gestured to her prioress for permission. Granted it, she stared down at the corpse for a long moment and scowled. "I do not recognize the fellow," she said. "He is not from one of our village families."

"Nor do I know his name, but that means little," the prioress said. "Many strangers have come here in recent times, some of whom I have had no cause to meet." She turned to her prior.

Andrew shook his head. "We could ask Mistress Gytha to come here and look upon the body."

Eleanor winced. Perhaps she should have asked her maid to accompany them. But the sight of this corpse would unbalance anyone's humors, and Gytha had been surprisingly downcast of late.

"She knows those in the village," the prior was saying, "and goes to market days as well as on visits to her brother." He looked down at the crowner and winked. "Others as well."

Ralf flushed and looked down at his hands. "No need for her to look on this." He rubbed his fingers together to brush off lumps of mud. "I've seen him. His name is Kenelm. Cuthbert said he came to Tyndal village last winter and remained. I know of no one here who will grieve over this death."

"Has he no family, then?" Eleanor gazed with fresh sorrow at the dead man.

"None that he claimed," Ralf said. "Nor does any woman here hold his bastard at her breast."

Sister Ruth lowered her gaze and glowered at a rock, suddenly deemed worthy of her displeasure.

"That is Kenelm?" Prior Andrew began to lean over the edge of the bank for a closer look, but his bad leg would not take his weight. He winced and stepped back. "I did meet him once. He came to the priory, seeking employment."

"Did you take him on?" The crowner raised an eyebrow in disbelief.

"I turned him away. We needed no one, and his manner was churlish. He looked fat enough, and I fear his demeanor made me disinclined to offer work out of simple charity."

"A wise decision, Prior. As I heard the tale, he was paid to guard some pilgrims traveling from the south to the shrine of Norwich's sainted William. When they arrived here, he fell ill." Ralf spat. "Or so he claimed. These pilgrims were simple souls and had given him all he demanded at the beginning of the journey, not at the end."

Sister Ruth snorted. "Surely they could require him to complete the work for which he had been contracted, or else demand return of the fee."

Ralf shrugged. "According to Cuthbert, they took pity on him in his sickness and let him keep the coins. And so they were left to travel without the protection of his stout cudgel. I hope God shielded those innocents, for they had little else to keep outlaws from feasting on their purses."

"To my knowledge, we never saw him at the hospital for any cure." Sister Ruth considered this for a moment. "I shall ask Brother Beorn, who might remember this low-born stranger." She spun around and glared at a lay brother but a short distance behind her.

Brother Gwydo seemed lost in prayer. Head lowered, his peaceful expression suggested his spirit was quite removed from the world in which he had found a corpse and this crime of murder. Then feeling the heat of her intense gaze, he started, bowed with respect, and asked how he might serve.

"Find Brother Beorn," she ordered. "Bring him to me immediately."

The man hurried off toward the hospital.

Ralf rubbed his face and stretched to see the banks of the pond above the mill wheel. A streak of damp mud now ran across his cheek like a scar.

"Why did Kenelm stay here? If he was known to cheat those who paid him, I wonder that anyone hired him," the prioress said.

"He earned enough for his bread," the crowner replied. "He did things other men would not."

Eleanor awaited his explanation.

"You recall the large parties of Jewish travelers that came through our village on their way to Norwich late last year and in the early spring?" Ralf looked down at the corpse.

"I do," Eleanor replied. "First, the Jews of Cambridge were cast from their homes at the command of the widowed Queen Eleanor, and then the exodus continued when King Edward ruled that all Jews could reside only in certain towns. Norwich was one."

"That Statute of Jewry!" Sister Ruth grumbled. "How could the king be so permissive? Imagine saying those people could even become farmers, thus taking land from Christian men."

The prioress bit her lip and ignored her sub-prioress. "We sorely missed your calming presence then, Crowner."

"I should have been here, but Sir Fulke needed every man he could get to provide the protection of the Jews that the king decreed. Had I remained in the village, perhaps this murder might not have occurred."

Sister Ruth's face grew mottled with the effort to remain silent.

"The Jews belong to the king," Andrew whispered to her. "He has the right to safeguard his property from harm."

She glared at him. Her disapproval of the king's protection was well known.

Eleanor felt herself growing warm, but not from the summer heat. "I do not understand. Was Kenelm involved in those matters?"

"Mistress Signy hired him during that time. She provided shelter and clean straw for the traveling Jews where she is now building more stables," Ralf said. "They would not eat the food cooked at her inn, for that was against their religion, but they were eager to pay for a dry place to sleep and the care she gave their animals."

"I recall that the families suffered theft along with other perils," Eleanor said. "Lawless men took advantage of them."

"That was why our innkeeper hired protection, adding the cost to her fee." The crowner touched the corpse with a toe.

"This fellow was the only man willing to rent his cudgel for a good price."

"Did he have occasion to use it?" The prioress looked grim.

"Once or twice on village men," Ralf said. "That did not gain him any friends."

"It probably gained him a few enemies," Eleanor said.

"Good Christian men, all," Sister Ruth snapped. "The inn-keeper should have turned the Jews away and let them sleep in the forest. If outlaws had fallen upon them, no one would have wept over the trials of such a stiff-necked people."

"King Edward ordered that they pass freely to those cities where they must return," Ralf replied with surprising sharpness. "No matter what you may think, the Statute refers to the will of the Holy Church that Jews be allowed to live unmolested. They have been under the English king's protection since the Conqueror invited them to come here from Rouen."

The sub-prioress turned her eyes heavenward.

Ralf hesitated, then seemed to think it best not to say more and instead bowed to the prioress. "I beg permission to leave this corpse in your priory, my lady. His death may fall under the king's law, but his soul belongs to God."

"Granted, Crowner," Eleanor replied. "We will prepare him for burial, of course. Should anything of interest be noted while we do so, we shall let you know immediately."

Pulling himself up and over the edge of the bank, Ralf stood and faced the prioress, a woman he called a friend. A grin twitched at the corners of his mouth. "As always, you are most kind in such matters."

Smiling at him, Eleanor turned to the assembled religious. "We must leave our crowner to investigate this murder." She raised her staff of office and started to walk away but after a short distance stepped aside and gestured for Prior Andrew to pass by. Motioning to Sister Ruth, she waited until the sub-prioress joined her.

"Whether or not Kenelm was a man of little merit or great," Eleanor said softly to the disgruntled nun, "he did not deserve an unlawful death. Even the wicked merit justice if the crime against them is unacceptable to both God and the king."

Sister Ruth pointed a finger over her shoulder in the direction of the corpse. "Kenelm's killer may be a godly man, my lady," she said, "and rightly offended if he was struck by a cudgel simply because he mocked a Jew. A good Christian is not at fault if God directs his hand against one who protects the wicked against the righteous."

"Whatever your thoughts in this matter, the death has nothing to do with us. Although the body was found here, it is a matter for the king's justice. It is up to Crowner Ralf to find the killer and up to God to judge the man's soul. And so you shall refrain from remarking any further on this death or on Kenelm. That is my command."

The sub-prioress muttered a barely civil promise.

"When Brother Beorn meets with you, you may tell him that I wish the body sent to Sister Anne. Should our good lay brother have any information bearing on this death, you are not to request details. He shall go immediately to inform the crowner and no one else."

Eleanor now took her sub-prioress by the arm and encouraged her to move swiftly along the path that led away from the corpse.

◇◇◇

Watching the two religious, the crowner smiled, suspecting what had passed between then. Then he sighed as he looked down at the swelling body in the mud. The investigation would be a weary one. His list of suspects included most of Tyndal village.

Chapter Four

Brother Thomas peered into the dark water of the mill pond. Sweat dripped into his eyes, and he carefully pressed a sleeve against them. Rubbing with the rough cloth only made the stinging worse.

Not that he regretted leaving his hermitage, but he did miss that easy access to a stream in summer where he could swim without being disturbed. A plunge into this pond was tempting.

Then he watched the gentle current rock thick green scum back and forth in the rushes. Wading in that rank vegetation would only transform him into a mortal version of some moss-like imp, a grass-colored creature with auburn hair who frolicked like a hungry fish in the pond. He imagined how that might frighten passers-by.

"Your smile suggests pleasant thoughts, Brother."

"Brother Gwydo! I did not see you." Thomas was startled but pleased over the unexpected encounter. Of late, he had found a rare ease in the lay brother's company and often sought the man for conversation or even a quiet time filled with companionable silence. Gwydo seemed equally content when they met.

"Would you share some ale with me? I was about to get my jug and escape to the shade of that tree." The lay brother gestured toward a small meadow bounded by fruit trees just off the path to the mill.

Grateful for the offer, Thomas nodded, knowing he could indulge in a few moments of peaceful company. Prioress Eleanor might have sent him to search for missed clues where Kenelm's corpse was found, but she had not required an immediate report of his findings.

Gwydo leapt effortlessly into the mud at the edge of the pond, then bent to retrieve a tan pottery flagon from a shaded patch of shallow water. With a grin, he swung the dripping object up for appreciative view.

"A hand?" Thomas reached out to help Gwydo up the bank.

The two men found a spot to sit where a slight breeze added cool comfort to the relief from the sun. The air was filled with a low hum as uncountable bees flew back and forth to their woven straw hives that were scattered throughout the open space.

"Have you had success with your skeps?" Thomas waved aside a dark insect only to realize it was probably a bee.

The lay brother gave the jug to the monk. "Well, I think the war of the kings has finished," he said.

"Of what war do you speak?"

"When the summer heat rises, the army of bees ascends like a black funnel, and they do battle. I was here, and it is a wonder to behold." His hands folded as if in prayer. "The king blows his horn. You can hear the tooting all through the meadow. Then he flies into the midst of his enemies like any brave and noble lord. You can hear the clicking of weapons and see the bodies of his victims fall to the ground. After the battle is done, the surviving bees and their victorious king return to the straw skeps I have woven. They now make honey for the priory." He smiled with loving delight. "Don't they sound peaceful?"

Thomas looked out at the many baskets, each placed wide-side down and sitting on a sturdy platform, and listened to the loud buzzing. The noise did not exactly signify tranquility to his ears. "All have foresworn combat?"

Gwydo pointed to one side of the hive collection. "Two groups remain querulous, but I think they will grow quiet in time. Do men not embrace peace after the violence of war? I would expect no less of bees."

The monk opted to take the lay brother's word on faith. "Many are grateful that you offered to do this task. I, for one, have no wish to get stung." He savored the cool bitterness of the ale, sighed, and passed the flagon back.

Gwydo drank, then ran his hand across his mouth. "Honey may taste sweeter after the bitterness of pain. Might that be an allegory for our life on earth and the rewards of heaven?"

Thomas suffered a chill of cruel memory. Was his life sweeter here because of his earlier imprisonment where even the rats mocked him? "Where did you learn this skill?" He hoped his voice did not betray his thoughts.

"In Outremer. Those golden bees made sure I suffered enough from their tiny swords, but these are good English black bees and rarely sting me." He looked at the skeps, his expression benign as he gazed on the busy creatures he tended.

"Perhaps God has told them that they must be kind because of your service as a pilgrim striving to restore Jerusalem to Christian hands."

"Or else they know I left my sword behind and returned unarmed. I am no menace to anyone, even these smallest creations of God."

Thomas met the man's gaze and smiled. If he was so easy in the lay brother's presence, he could understand why the bees might feel equally comfortable with him.

"But I do not think you came here to speak of bees, Brother." Gwydo chuckled as he again passed the jug, "Nor do I think you were on your way to serve God in the village. You rarely linger to stare into the mill pond even on hot days when you have a purpose to fulfill."

Thomas leaned his head back against the rough bark. "The memory of your performance as Daniel in the Christmas drama gives pleasure all year. Perhaps I had hoped to hear you sing again, even if it was only to those buzzing creatures."

Gwydo smiled. "You are good to say so, but my time for vanity is long past."

"My praise was honestly spoken."

"Then your words are soft in my ears even if your reason for speaking them was intended to disguise your true purpose here."

Thomas grinned. "You mean I longed for a cool draught of your ale?"

"Nay, good brother." His expression grew solemn as he leaned forward and embraced his knees. "Your reputation is well known. If a crime has been committed, men pray that Prioress Eleanor and Brother Thomas will be nigh to render justice. I have less trust in our crowner, although I've been told he is both clever and honest."

Thomas flushed at the compliment. Perhaps his own time for vanity had not quite passed. "I do not spend my days longing for murders to solve." He hoped to suggest humility, but the eagerness he heard in those words betrayed a lust for adventure that was unsuitable in a pious monk.

"Nor does our prioress, but Death follows you both like a pup of that legendary, hell-spawned, black hound from Norfolk."

Without warning, Gwydo began gasping.

"Are you ill?" Thomas grabbed the man's shoulder.

The lay brother shook his head, managed a shallow breath, then another. Although his face was scarlet, he looked relieved. "Fear not. The moment is over. I live." He was wheezing badly. "Sister Anne feared I had the lung disease when I first came to this priory. Now she thinks otherwise. Only in summer do I suffer these moments…" He coughed. "And I do fear I will suffocate."

Thomas jumped up. "Shall I summon a lay brother from the hospital? Or does Sister Anne have a potion I could bring for relief?"

Shaking his head, Gwydo gestured for the monk to sit. "Your company is all I need. Please stay. In a moment, I will be well enough to stand." He sucked in more air. "And then I shall take you to…where I found the body…and answer any questions you might have." This time the breath he took was a deeper one, and his eyes grew bright with relief. "But only if you wish to do so."

"I should not trouble you with my idle curiosity."

"I welcome the distraction from my mortal afflictions and long to offer a small service to the cause of justice."

Thomas opened his mouth to protest but quickly saw that the man meant what he had said. "If the bees will not miss your warrior's skill, should they have plans for a future battle, I would be grateful."

Gwydo stretched his hand out, and the monk pulled him to his feet. The lay brother's hand was rough, Thomas thought, but his grip was so gentle. Then fearing he had held the man's hand an instant too long, he drew back and folded his arms into his sleeves.

"We may leave the bees to the labors they understand better than we," Gwydo said, his tone showing no hint of disapproval. He motioned for the monk to follow him.

As they approached the bank of the mill pond, the lay brother pointed to a particular spot in the rushes. "I found the body when I went to sink my jug into the cool water," he said. "The man called Kenelm was floating here."

"You believed he had drowned?"

"I prayed he was still alive, but, when I reached him, I saw that his throat had been cut. I had no doubt he had been murdered." He bit his lip. "Killed by another, that is. No man wishing to commit self-murder could cut so deeply."

Thomas caught something in the man's tone. To make such a distinction, he suspected the lay brother had known fellow soldiers so anguished in spirit or physical pain that an eternity in Hell seemed preferable to a moment longer of life. Had Gwydo given some the solace of death, as he heard others had done for their comrades? He shook the questions from his mind. "What did you do after you knew the man's death was a violent one?"

Gwydo hesitated. "I did not rush to tell Prioress Eleanor, if that is what you meant. Although I am not an expert in these matters, I did consider whether or not the killer was still nearby."

Surprised, Thomas stared at the man. "You surely did not seek him out with no weapon to protect yourself?"

"I am cautious by nature and stealthy by practice, Brother. Having learned to slip up on the beast with which I longed to fill my empty belly, I can walk silently enough to hunt a man."

"And did you find anything of interest?" The monk tried to conceal his surprise at hearing an unexpected coldness in the man's voice.

"No killer waited for me to catch him, so I then hurried to alert our prioress."

"And later?"

"You have caught me out, Brother." Gwydo slapped the monk on his shoulder. "I was not satisfied when Crowner Ralf said the deed must have been committed outside our walls. Had he included our grounds in his search for clues, I would have been content. He did not. I found that troubling."

Thomas nodded. Prioress Eleanor was equally unwilling to let that conclusion lie without challenge, but he did not say so aloud. Although she had no quarrel with the crowner, it was her duty to make sure there was no doubt about jurisdiction between secular and religious authority.

"After I sent Brother Beorn to our sub-prioress, I again abandoned the bees and perused the bank above the mill. Come with me up the path and see what I found." Gesturing for the monk to follow, he strode off.

Thomas noticed that Gwydo now breathed with ease. As he followed along the banks, he realized how little he knew of this lay brother, a man who had arrived at the priory with a high fever and a festering wound from which no one expected him to survive. Many deemed his recovery a miracle so none were amazed when he begged entry to the priory as a lay brother. Thomas had also learned that Gwydo was once a crusader. That such a man, weary of war and cured by God's grace, would eagerly take vows did not surprise the monk. What did was the latent excitement this new and fatal violence seemed to have awakened in Gwydo.

Thomas found that both interesting and troubling in a man, unlike himself, who was truly pious.

Gwydo had stopped. "There," he gestured as if the significance was obvious.

Thomas studied the path to the gate that led toward the village, noting only that the grass between path and stream was well-trampled. "Many travel this way," he said and confessed that he failed to see what the lay brother meant.

"But they don't leave blood." Gwydo asked the monk to come closer, then knelt in the grass at the edge of the stream just above where it flowed over the wheel into the pond below.

Thomas crouched beside him and frowned. "Now I see. Someone has pulled up the grass and weeds here." Then he bent closer to look at the spot indicated by Gwydo. He dug his fingers into the earth, and, when he looked at his hand, he saw stains of a rust color. "Blood," he confirmed.

"I think the victim was killed here," Gwydo said. "Then he fell or perhaps he was pushed into the stream."

Thomas sat back. "Neither Cuthbert nor the crowner have seen this?"

"To my knowledge, neither examined this area. As I said, the crowner believes the killing took place beyond the priory and is probably still looking for evidence upstream."

Thomas looked toward the gate. "Why did you not send word to our prioress?"

"The bells rang for the last office. I obeyed them to offer prayers. I found you here soon after returning."

The explanation was reasonable. As Thomas recalled, both he and the prioress had missed the office due to their discussion of Kenelm's death. "Crowner Ralf's conclusion about how the body arrived in the pond would have been plausible had this killing only been a quarrel between angry mortals." He looked sadly at Gwydo. "But no man would blacken his soul by killing a man here for such a petty matter. Shedding blood in the priory violates the sanctity of God's ground. This evidence suggests the crime may be a far darker one than any have thought."

Gwydo drew back, his expression inscrutable. "I fear that you and our prioress will be drawn into investigating after all."

Thomas rose to his feet and brushed the dust off his robe. "Prioress Eleanor may not be pleased that the crime has ceased to be the king's sole problem, but she will thank you for discovering this."

As he glanced again at Gwydo, however, he caught a fleeting look in the man's eyes that made him uneasy. In a man he thought so gentle, he was quite sure he had seen a flicker of hate.

Chapter Five

Ralf gulped his dark ale, ran a hand across his mouth, and belched. "Will you sit with me?" he asked, looking up at the golden-haired, buxom woman standing across from him. Sheepishly, he smiled.

Signy, the innkeeper, folded her hands. The gesture suggested a virtuous femininity, as did her simple black robe, but the corners of her eyes crinkled with merriment, revealing that she was well-accustomed to the vagaries of men. From this fleeting hint, the wise would know that any who tried to deceive her would, at the very least, suffer deep wounds from her wit's sharp edge.

"I do not sit with those who drink at my inn, Crowner. Gossip feeds on such things in the village."

"Surely nothing would be said if you spent a few moments with me?" He spread his hands. "I am an old friend, Signy."

"Friend? I might once have granted you that title, but you have long since lost the right. Now you ask to speak with me only when murder has been committed." Her eyes narrowed. "It is not my virtue for which I fear but rather my neck."

He hit the table with his fist. "Will you never forgive…?"

Sliding onto the bench opposite him, Signy bent closer and whispered: "Not ever, Ralf." She quickly leaned back with a hearty laugh. "Now what do you seek?"

The crowner took refuge in his ale, deliberately savoring the remaining drops as an excuse not to acknowledge all the meanings hidden behind the intense blue of her eyes. "A killer," he muttered after hesitating too long.

"Whose?" Signy's tone announced that she had ceased jesting.

"Kenelm's body was found in the priory mill pond this morning. His throat was cut."

The news caused a flutter of surprise to cross her face. "No one will weep when he hears that news," she said. "I pray the killer did not have just cause for his deed, else many will protest his hanging for it."

"I know he was disliked, yet he must not have been without some merit. You told me you had hired him when the Jews traveled through here on their way to Norwich after their expulsion from nearby towns."

"And hired him again when another small party of them arrived a few nights ago." She shook her head with contempt. "You speak of merit, but Kenelm's merit lay solely in his broad shoulders, strong cudgel, and deep love for shiny coin. Many in this village have no tolerance for the Jews. Since my wages were high enough, he was willing to guard them against injury and theft."

The Crowner scowled. "Why is there so much ill-will here against the king's people? They have never lived in Tyndal, nor are they ever like to do so. No one has suffered from their practice of usury. Men of higher rank were the ones to quarrel with the Jews over debts, not ones like our blacksmith, Hob, or the new wheelwright."

Signy glanced quickly over her shoulder. "As I learned from a merchant passing through, the king ordered that the Jews give up usury and earn their bread by other labor. One of his unfortunate suggestions seems to have been that they might toil in the fields. The rumor spreads that Christians will be forced to sell or even give up land and other property to them without due recompense. One fisherman has hidden his boat so he won't have to surrender it."

"That is untrue! When King Edward declared that the Jews might *take* land, he meant that they could buy it with proper compensation and only from willing sellers. No one will be forced to give up anything."

"Then you know the exact words of this statute?"

He nodded. "When I was in Norwich, my brother and I discussed the implications at length. It was our duty to administer the statute as the king intended."

"The villagers are not so well informed, Ralf, and, as you should know, good sense rarely wins after rumor surrounds men with thick walls of fear."

Lifting his pitch-coated leather jack, Ralf swallowed the last of his ale and stared around the inn. Other than the pilgrims and traveling merchants, he knew the men here, some from childhood but the rest for years enough to know they were neither better nor worse than God's average creation. And that meant they were as capable of hate as they were of love.

He rubbed his hand over his bristled cheeks and turned back to the innkeeper. "Yet you gave safe haven to the Jews on their way to Norwich. Why not tell them to pass on, that there was no room in your inn?"

Signy did not reply and turned instead to gesture to a boy who was carefully transporting a jug through the crowd. The child nodded in acknowledgement, delivered his burden, and quickly wove through the groups of men to her side.

"Bring our crowner a half jug of the best ale, Nute," she said and smiled at her foster child.

"I would be most grateful." Ralf added a comradely wink.

Blushing with happiness, the boy disappeared.

Ralf looked back at Signy and waited to see if she would reply to his question or continue to avoid the subject.

She was studying him with amusement. "It is time you married again and had a son of your own, Crowner."

He was not ready for this. Turning scarlet, Ralf croaked a protest.

"Shush." She swatted at him as if waving aside a fly. "Do not prove yourself more of a fool than I know you are. If you do not soon take Mistress Gytha to wife, she will wed a merchant who will thumb his nose at you as he takes her far away. You have delayed unreasonably, and the maiden is too worthy to remain unwed much longer."

The crowner's mouth became too dry for speech.

Signy held his gaze for a long moment, then she twisted around to watch Nute at the far side of the inn. When she looked back, her eyes had softened. "That boy and his sister are my joys," she murmured. "He is eager to learn the business of inn-keeping. I have just set him the work of collecting empty pitchers for cleaning and bringing the occasional order of small jugs."

"A good'un you have." Ralf said and waited for his answer. Signy had delayed long enough to consider her reply.

"You asked why I housed Jews when the village would have praised me for telling them to sleep in the outlaw-infested woodland instead."

Ralf knew Signy had meant no harm with that sharp jab about Gytha, but he also suspected she was uneasy over the question about the Jews. The concern for her friend may have come from the heart, but it had also succeeded in putting him off-balance and less able to pry when she did answer his question. He quietly forgave the stratagem and nodded.

Signy tilted her head and let silence again fall between them. After a quick glance to see who might be seated nearby, she leaned closer to reply. "They asked only for shelter from the bitter wind and dry straw on which to sleep one night." She studied the palm of her hand. "God has blessed me with prosperity, and I had just bought much of the land surrounding this inn, before their exodus to Norwich, but could do little with it because of the winter season."

Nute suddenly appeared at Ralf's side, his expression grave as he lifted the jug as high as he could. The crowner quickly relieved him of his burden and whispered thanks in the lad's ear, taking the opportunity to slip a shiny object into the small fist. Nute grinned and rushed off, carefully avoiding Signy's eyes.

"That coin was unnecessary, Crowner, but any gift from you is cherished. He'll save it, not spend." Pressing a finger into the corner of one eye, she smiled. "He worships you."

For all the sins he had committed against this woman in the past, cruelties she had reasons never to forgive, he knew he would always be bonded to Signy in ways undefined by any known word. Nute had certainly earned a place in his heart, but any kindness he showed the lad was meant for this woman as well.

She blinked, as if a dust mote had stung her eyes, and then stiffened her back. "In brief, Crowner, I saw something to gain from their need and charged them for each service. I hired a guard to keep them safe, their animals were cared for, and I offered wine to banish the cold. For all this, I found profit in land that would be otherwise useless until spring. To anyone who criticizes me in this, I reply that my actions were nothing more than good business."

"Or else it was charity," Ralf whispered.

Signy gripped her hands until the knuckles turned bone-white.

Although her quiet kindness to the unfortunate had made her beloved in the village, he was sure she must have been condemned, her faith even questioned, for sheltering a despised people. This was not the first time he had cause to admire her courage.

Leaning forward, the inn-keeper replied, her voice so soft he could barely hear the words: "I will tell you this, my Lord Crowner. Never once did a Jew feel up a serving woman, vomit on my floor from too much drink, or fail to pay what was owed and with courtesy. There are many Christian men for whom I could not say the same."

"I must still ask why you hired Kenelm to be a guard, a man known to cheat and, aye, steal from honest men."

"I never paid him until he performed the task, and I paid him more than he could get elsewhere. Had I found any other man willing to do the work, I would never have hired him."

"And you again asked him to do the same for these latest arrivals, a group that must have hurried on by now for they have long delayed obedience to the king's orders." He frowned. Need he chase after these people and investigate that matter, too?

"The family of Jacob ben Asser is still here, and I shall be hard-pressed to promise them safety now that Kenelm is dead." The innkeeper sighed. "They cannot travel yet."

"And the cause for this?"

"The wife is close to term in her pregnancy. Giving birth on the road to Norwich, without any skilled woman to aid in the labor, would be dangerous for both babe and mother."

Ralf shuddered as if the ghost of his own wife, who died after childbirth, had just laid an icy hand on the back of his neck. "Sister Anne..."

"I mentioned her skills, but the husband will not allow his child and wife to be tended by a nun. I may have to help the woman myself, inexperienced as I am, even though I must swear not to christen the newborn in secret." Her mouth tightened.

"I shall tell Cuthbert to protect the family," he said.

"I am grateful. He will be reliable. Kenelm was not, although I now know he may have been dead when he did not arrive for the work two nights ago."

Ralf noted that fact. "Did he fail to appear on other occasions?" Perhaps that answer would reveal some pathway to solving this crime. With luck, he might discover that Kenelm did have a woman...

Signy's lips formed a thin smile. "In the winter, he would sometimes fail to arrive, later claiming it was too cold for him or the pay was not enough to suffer villager abuse. If thefts occurred, or other damage done, I refunded money paid for protection. With this family, however, he was quite reliable but took especial pleasure in mocking them for their faith. I often heard the husband shouting at him."

Ralf lifted his jack of ale and quickly downed the contents to ease his growing discontent. The list of suspects had just increased.

Chapter Six

Prioress Eleanor crouched on the bank by the mill pond and brushed her fingers through the grass.

"It was there." The monk pointed to a spot just to the left of her hand.

Sister Anne watched, hoping that Brother Thomas would be wrong for once.

The prioress dug into the ground and brought up a handful of russet-colored earth.

"Might the blood have come from a wild animal?" The sub-infirmarian's expression suggested she already knew the answer to her own question.

"The high walls keep them out," the prioress said, "although some might still slip in." She bent over to look more closely at the place where Thomas believed grass had been pulled up. "If I am not mistaken, that is a footprint." She gestured for the two monastics to view the mark in the ground.

Sister Anne nodded. "Some force was required to make that deep a gouge."

"I saw it, my lady," Thomas said, "but concluded it might have been made at any time."

Eleanor stood. "In that, I would agree, for this is a well-worn path, but we had a heavy summer downpour late the day before last. Gytha said that kept her from returning earlier. This print is both distinct and deep, which suggests it was recently made, when the earth was still wet."

"Few would step off the path after that rain. The mud would be slippery and a misstep might cause someone to fall into the water," Anne replied.

The prioress considered the possibilities in that, then shook her head. "A man might slip into the pond and drown but not slit his throat while doing it."

"That patch." Thomas bent down and sketched a wide circle above the spot with his hand. "I think the killer and Kenelm struggled there. In fact, I'd say those were heel marks near the footprint."

Eleanor frowned. "Or else the body was dragged off the path. See those marks over there. Yet we cannot prove whether a fight occurred or something quite benign."

"I think he was killed here. That patch of blood would suggest it." Thomas walked to the edge of the bank and looked into the water. "It is not far from here to the mill wheel."

"We must tell Ralf about this," Anne said. "If Cuthbert has found no stronger evidence upstream to prove where Kenelm went into the water, the sergeant might not have to look further than this place."

"I have sent Brother Beorn to seek out our crowner." Shading her eyes, Eleanor gazed down the path. The gate into the priory was not far from the mill, allowing villagers to carry their grain with ease from the road that passed by.

She frowned and turned to the sub-infirmarian. "You have looked at Kenelm's corpse. If the murder took place here, so close to the mill, surely the dead body would have been found sooner. Ralf thinks the body was in the water for a couple of days. Might the death have occurred outside our priory as he believes?"

"I agree with Ralf about the length of time the body was in the water. Although there were cuts on Kenelm's face, our crowner did not see the ones on his back. I cannot be sure about the cause, but they could mean his body was trapped by something underwater and only went over the mill wheel when the current finally pulled it loose."

"Might those hidden marks have been caused by a fight?"

"The ones on his face perhaps," the nun replied, "but the scrapes on his back suggest that something large hit him several times. If the body was trapped under the wheel, that would explain those wounds."

"We must ask why anyone would kill another here." Thomas looked around. "It is a crime only the impious or the mad would commit."

They fell silent, and Eleanor felt cold despite the hot day. The monk was right, and she feared the answer.

Tyndal Priory had suffered violence within its walls before, but surely God's servants had given Him no cause to curse them again. She required all her monks and nuns to obey the Rule on diet, labor, and prayer. The priory was respected for charity given and vows kept. Her own private transgressions she acknowledged and did hard penance. All mortals sinned, but, as far as she knew, her religious were no worse than those in other pious communities. Why must this priory endure so much bloodshed?

As if to belie the gravity of blood spilled on sacred ground, peace felt as tangible to Eleanor as this dense heat. She looked up at the sky. A growing number of clouds scudded overhead, hinting that another summer cloudburst was imminent. Birdsong was muted. Leaves rustled briefly as a sudden gust of sea breeze brought a hint of coolness down from the northern regions. If God were so angry, wouldn't He give her some sign, something to point out the offense that must be corrected?

The prioress looked back at her two companions, regretting the question she must ask. "Do either of you know whether any of our monks, lay or choir, might have had a quarrel with Kenelm?"

"None of whom I was aware," Thomas replied. He looked at Anne.

"Those within these walls had little opportunity to suffer injury from him. The dead man only arrived here after the harvest was taken in," the nun said. "As our crowner suggested,

Kenelm was not well-loved by the villagers who did have contact with him. I never met the man, but I have overheard resentful comments about him made by some coming to us for care."

"Since his arrival, have any of our religious been given leave to go outside our walls?" Thomas asked.

Eleanor denied it.

"I have, and I never met him," he said.

"When the lay brothers brought the body to the hospital, those who saw it assumed he was a traveler found dead on the road." Anne paused for a moment. "Not all dwelling in our priory did see the corpse, but our nuns are sequestered and we have few monks."

"Brother Gwydo is the only one who has not been here long," Eleanor said.

Thomas shook his head. "Surely he could not have had anything to do with this."

"It is unlikely, Brother," Sister Anne said. "He has only just recovered enough strength to oversee the honey production, a light enough task for him. I do not think he would have been able to kill a man as strong as Kenelm, even if he had had cause."

"There was the blow to the head," the monk said, his reluctance in mentioning this quite evident. "If Kenelm was stunned, a weaker man could have cut his throat."

"Brother Thomas and I examined the body." Anne turned to Eleanor. "I concluded that the skull may have been cracked, but the blow did not kill him. Why the killer did not strike him again but instead cut his throat is a fair question."

"The murderer wanted to make sure he was dead?" Thomas looked doubtful. "He was so angry he both struck him and cut his throat?"

"It is odd to do both. A man suffering frenzy will stab more than once, if he uses a knife, or hit his victim repeatedly, if he first struck him," Anne said. "We know very little, in fact. I grieve that I could not find anything of especial note from my examination. I doubt the corpse has more to teach us."

"Then we shall bury him," Eleanor replied. In the summer heat, quick burial was obligatory. Out of the corner of her eye, she glanced at Sister Anne.

After their return from Baron Herbert's castle last winter, the sub-infirmarian had grown gaunt. Now, for the first time, there was a healthy blush in Anne's cheeks and a long absent interest hovering in her eyes. "Your observations may own more merit than you think. I am grateful, and our crowner shall be as well," the prioress said, feeling relief at the change in her friend.

Thomas, on the other hand, looked uneasy. "Do you still believe this matter belongs to the king's justice?"

"The crime was committed on priory land," Eleanor said. "Although we may feel confident that none of our religious were involved, I must still look more deeply into the question. Even if all of us are innocent, I must be kept informed and may wish to assist our crowner." She smiled. "Ralf has always welcomed our assistance, so we shall freely offer our help."

"But why did the crime occur at this spot?" Thomas rubbed sweat off his forehead. "It is but a short walk to the gate. If a quarrel burst out between two men, they would have left the priory to settle their differences. The forest or the road would have been the most likely place to fight. Why shed blood on God's earth?"

"Like you, I am troubled by that," Eleanor replied. Her gray eyes now matched the color of the darkening clouds. "I fear murder was not done within our walls by accident. There was a reason."

Chapter Seven

Belia squeezed her mother's arm with all her strength. Sweat ran down her face in rivulets.

Ignoring the pain of her daughter's grip, Malka crooned to her with soft love, although she had just looked with dark anger at her son-in-law, Jacob ben Asser.

The young woman could not have owned more than twenty summers on earth, but her features resembled those of an ancient crone, sharp-edged and hollow-cheeked. When she opened her eyes, terror glittered from them. Death's touch was one all mortals know. Belia stood at the edge of a grave and knew the space would fit her well.

"Sleep, my dove," the mother said. "The pain shall pass. This is but any woman's trial. Did I not bear you and your three brothers?" She shrugged. "And here I sit beside you, no worse for it all. You will soon forget this labor when the babe lies safely in your arms. That, I promise." Smiling, she kissed her daughter's cheek.

Belia nodded weakly, her jaw briefly setting with determination before her eyelids, once again, grew too heavy. The pain must have lessened. She fell into an uneasy sleep.

Slipping away from her child's loosening grasp, Malka rose and motioned for Jacob to step away from the large-bellied woman who was his suffering wife.

They walked just outside the stall, more suited to housing a horse than three adults. One young servant leapt to her feet in anticipation of some request. Jacob shook his head and asked her to stand some distance away so he and his mother-in-law might speak in private.

"She needs more than I can give her," Malka said.

"And you are all she has," he replied in a broken whisper. From his eyes, tears rolled down his smooth-shaven cheeks like a flash-flood. He gestured discreetly at the servant. "That one is but a child."

"Tell me how I shall aid her in birth with these?" The mother stretched forth her hands. The fingers were bent, some backwards and others sideways, the knuckles were huge, and the skin red. "I would kill her and the babe, even if I had the strength to pull the child into the world. She needs a midwife."

"Had we reached Norwich, we'd have had our choice of skilled women." He pointed toward the opening in the unfinished wall. "Here we are surrounded by those who hate us." He grimaced. "The innkeeper offered to send for a nun. A nun! One who would have baptized the child, stolen the babe before he could suck his own mother's milk, and passed him to a Christian family to raise. How…" He buried his head in his hands.

Malka turned away, her jaw set with anger, looking much as her daughter had before falling asleep.

From inside the stall, Belia whimpered, and the mother now lost her resolve as well. Tears wound their way through the creases in her cheeks.

Jacob put his arm around her shoulders. She rested her head on his.

Quietly, the two wept.

From outside the partially completed stable, a man's voice suddenly roared. "Let the scales of the Devil's blindness drop from your eyes. Listen to God's Will. Hear His Son's cry. Be not a stiff-necked people and embrace the truth! Accept baptism. Be saved from Hell!"

The young servant cried out and braced herself against the wall, her widening eyes black with helpless terror.

A cry of anguish escaping from his lips, Jacob leapt to his feet.

His mother-in-law tried to grab his robe, but her hand found only air. "Do not go out there!"

Jacob looked down at her, fury turning his face as bright as fire. "No sooner do I rid us of one abuser than another takes his place. I will kill him!"

She took a deep breath. "Stay calm," she whispered. "We dare not fight back, except with reason and gentle courtesy."

"Those who scream such things at us own neither," he hissed.

Again the man outside shouted: "Cease your dance with the Devil and accept the cleansing of baptism. Your willful denial of His truth corrupts all you touch. How long do you think God and good Christian men will tolerate this before you are destroyed like the evil ones in Sodom and Gomorrah?"

From the stall, Belia groaned.

Jacob put the heel of his hands against his eyes, then threw his head back and shook his fist at the door leading to the inn yard. "I cannot allow that fool to destroy what little peace my wife has! She bears a child. If she must do so in a horse stall with neither a gentle midwife nor a decent bed in which to nurse the babe, surely she should be allowed to sleep without this bellowing."

Malka looked up at him, and her expression changed to weary resignation. "If you must go forth, do so with humility and a calm voice. Men who shout condemnation at us often hold swords and pitchforks with which to pierce our breasts, but a meek man has been known to soften even a lion's heart. If you leave here with fist raised, you court death as surely as if you faced a wild beast. Shall your child never know his father?"

"All I want is for him to cease his ranting. Belia must gather her strength." Jacob groaned. "But you are right. Shall I promise to listen to his preaching after the child is born? In Cambridge, I was forced to do so once a week. Another few hours of that is worth an hour of quiet for my wife."

"And speak of charity, on your knees if you must, and say that you will ponder his words. Beg him for merciful compassion while you do." Malka ran her hand along the seam of her robe as if considering the quality of the stitches. "Christians think they invented the virtue," she said, glancing back at Jacob with a quick smile. "If it helps us all survive, let the man outside continue to believe it."

Jacob bent down to kiss the top of his mother-in-law's head. "It shall be as you say. You are wiser than I shall ever be." His voice was soft with love for this woman, one who had not only given birth to his adored wife but had also embraced him as a son after his own mother had died.

Then he straightened, touched the yellow badge sewn on his robes by the order of King Edward, and walked out into the courtyard.

Chapter Eight

Ralf strode from the inn. The sun was bright in his eyes, but his mood darkened as he looked down the road at the crowds milling around the merchant stalls.

It was marketing day, a time for families to visit with friends and see what wondrous things had come with Norwich merchants or even from Cambridge. Women argued with butchers, men debated the merits of one tradesman's wares over another's, and laughing children ran around the legs of all.

A father holding his laughing son caught the crowner's particular attention. He rubbed a hand over his eyes.

Signy was right. Although he loved his daughter to distraction, he had yet to remarry and produce an heir as he had promised his eldest brother. Fulke's wife had long been barren, yet the man refused to find cause to divorce her, a choice that had warmed Ralf's heart for just an instant. And in that regrettable moment of weakness, he had given his word that he would produce the requisite, legitimate heir as long as his next wife was of his own choosing.

Ever since, he had found innumerable reasons to avoid keeping that ill-advised oath. The problem was not in making his choice of wife. He knew the woman he would ask, but approaching his friend, Tostig, for permission to marry his sister made Ralf tremble like a virgin on the wedding night. He had grown to love Gytha; indeed he adored her too much.

A cloud passed over the sun, and the daylight faded to match his grayer mood.

He had already suffered rejection from the last woman he longed to marry for more years than he dared count. First, she had chosen another over him, then God. As for his late wife, she had been a good woman, but there had been no love between them. She had died birthing their daughter.

He shook his head and concluded that it was not only prudent for him to reject ties with all women, they were wise to avoid him as well. In silence he complained to God, protesting that He should never have created Eve. That apple aside, Adam's life would have been far less complicated without her.

The question always came down to this: why would Gytha want to join with such a rough man as he? She was tenderhearted; he had grown cynical. Although he had some wealth, she could find merchants with softer ways and more coin than he. In short, he had nothing to offer, apart from one promise never take her away from the village she loved and another to worship the earth wherever she set her feet.

Maybe she would consent if he phrased his plea as a kindness to his daughter, a child she loved as much as if she had borne Sibely herself. But his throat went dry when he tried to ask and the words died in his mouth. Another opportunity would pass. He feared Gytha would flee if he told her how much he loved her, and his daughter would lose the warmth of the maid's love. He did not dare chance that.

But today he had intended an innocent outing with Gytha. All he had planned to do was carry her basket while she shopped for Prioress Eleanor's table. Oh, he had hoped to surprise her with a small gift as well, but only to thank her for the happiness she brought his daughter. At no point would he even hint at how much joy her company brought him too.

He growled like a cornered dog. Instead of an enjoyable afternoon, he had a murder to solve, and a popular one at that. Gytha's pleasant image fled his soul, replaced by that of a butchered corpse.

He knew no one would cooperate and could already hear the village response to his queries: "'Twas a stranger that did it, Crowner! I swear I saw him, dagger in hand, running down the road. Why did I not stop him? Do you think me daft? He had a knife! Do I remember how he looked? Maybe short. Brown hair, perhaps light, nay, dark…"

Ralf cursed. Now he must talk with the Jewish family and decide if their quarrel with Kenelm was sharp enough for a killing. And the wife was close to giving birth? He did not like this situation at all.

Then he remembered he had offered to loan the innkeeper his sergeant to guard this family. His spirit instantly brightened. He could leave the inquiry of them to Cuthbert!

As if called in answer to his prayer, the sergeant walked around the corner from the inn. Ralf began to smile, then felt his stomach fill with fire. Either the man's grim expression meant something unpleasant, or else that last jack of ale he had drunk with the innkeeper had been unwise.

Cuthbert raised a hand in greeting. "Brother Beorn met me on the road and sent news you must hear."

Ralf grunted.

"Brother Gwydo and Brother Thomas found blood that suggests Kenelm was killed on priory grounds."

Kicking a stone with such force that it almost hit a passing villager in the back, Ralf uttered a colorful oath.

"Need I continue looking upstream? I have found nothing of value and…"

"I have another task for you, one that will better merit your time." Looking back at the inn, Ralf wondered how much of that good ale was still left. As he considered the implications of this new information, the prospect of another jug of the inn's finest regained appeal. "As for the priory, I had hoped not to trouble them with this death."

"Prioress Eleanor also sent word that she would meet with you and shall assist as much as possible."

"Which means she will investigate the matter herself if she suspects the involvement of any of her religious."

Cuthbert nodded, his expression wisely void of meaning.

"I will seek an audience with her later," Ralf said. At least the visit might bring him a moment with Gytha. "Come." He put a hand on his sergeant's shoulder and aimed him along the path leading to the partially completed stables behind the inn.

As they rounded the corner of the building, however, they came to an abrupt halt.

A young man knelt in front of the unfinished stable, the entrance to which was draped with stiff cloth. Waving his arms at the sky, he shouted pleas for the salvation of the souls within the shelter.

The rough covering was shoved aside and a man emerged. He stared down at the praying youth as if perplexed by his behavior. "My wife is ill," he said, then humbly bowed his head. "You have awakened her. In the name of all you hold sacred, have mercy and leave us in peace." He coughed sharply, as if something had caught in his throat, before adding: "Would it not be charitable to do so?"

The youth glared at the man in disgust and clasped his hands together into a doubled fist. The cross around his neck wobbled as his body trembled with the intensity of his passion. "Charity? Why do you think you are owed such a thing, unbelievers that you are? If you turn from your benighted faith, open your wicked hearts to Our Lord's message and let Him save you from eternal damnation, I shall leave you in peace to enjoy the blessing of His salvation. Charity is only for those who see or seek the Truth. All others must suffer misery for that is the only thing eternity has to offer you."

"I have not come to argue faith, only to ask that you let my wife sleep." The man's voice grew taut with controlled rage.

"Of what value is sleep when she faces the fires of Hell?"

The man's face turned white.

Ralf walked up to the lad and placed a hand on his shoulder. "Your father needs you, Adelard. Rise and attend him."

"In this matter, God the Father outranks any earthly parent…"

"Still you must honor Oseberne the baker. Of that there is no dispute."

"Our Lord said…"

"As crowner of this land, Adelard, I order you to leave this place and seek your father." None too gently, Ralf grabbed the youth by his robe and hauled him to his feet. "Off with you!" Then he shoved him in the direction of the market stalls.

Cuthbert watched the youth stagger off and began to laugh. "Your tongue has taken vows, methinks. A priest could have not have preached a better…"

Ignoring his sergeant, Ralf spoke to the man who remained standing before him. "I am the crowner here. This misbegotten oaf is my sergeant."

"I am called Jacob ben Asser, lately of Cambridge but now returning to Norwich, a permitted *archa* town, as King Edward and his noble mother have ordered."

"A belated journey to go back to those places where the records of your people's usury are kept," Ralf said. He nodded at the badge of yellow taffeta, six fingers long and three wide, shaped like the Tablets of the Law and sewn on the man's clothes above his heart. "Others of your faith have obeyed the royal commands with greater alacrity."

Jacob said nothing.

Studying his face, Ralf discovered nothing that revealed what the young man thought. They must suck in caution with their mothers' milk, he mused. How different it had been when he was a boy and traveled with his father whose duties often took him to Norwich. Jewish and Christian children played together with some freedom until they reached a certain age… He blinked away the memory.

Jacob met his gaze. "My wife's uncle fell ill and died just when we received word that we must leave Cambridge. It took time to arrange …"

"There is a Jewish cemetery in Cambridge. Unlike others of your faith living elsewhere, you had no permits to request, extra fees to pay, or a long journey."

"Forgive me, my lord. There were special problems. We tried to summon his children for mourning but, by then, they were told they must leave for *archa* towns under the statute. As quickly as possible, we had to sell what could be and organize safe conduct for the widow to travel to Lincoln, the *archa* town to which her daughter and her son-in-law had gone at the king's command."

Ralf started to speak.

Jacob anticipated the presumed question. "I did not have the requisite license to stay in Cambridge, but I have proof that I paid the proper fee for the right to remain there until now." His voice betrayed no resentment.

Ralf glared. His roughness of manner would not surprise this man and would also let the crowner hide his thoughts. In fact, he hated the Statute of Jewry. Courtiers had long howled over debts they owed Jewish moneylenders, debts made more onerous because of royal policies that required greater speed in repayment. Now that Edward had turned to Italian merchants for his own needs, instead of relying on the Jews, he could gain favor with his barons by eliminating future usurious loans, hampering repayment of past ones, and putting harsher restrictions on a despised group.

The crowner felt some sympathy for the king's people, and most certainly resented the extra work the statute caused sheriffs, but none of this would he admit to Jacob ben Asser, a man who might be a murderer. "You travel with your wife. Others?"

The man gestured toward the unfinished stables. "One maidservant and my mother-in-law. The others were sent ahead to seek lodging for us all in Norwich, along with the armed men we had hired for protection on the road."

A mewling cry came from the hut.

All Jacob's determination to remain impassive melted. He began to wring his hands. "My wife is heavy with child, my lord. She suffers greatly and cannot travel the last distance to Norwich. If you will, accept payment in exchange for permission to remain…"

"Keep your coin. I want it not," Ralf snapped. "As for the health of your wife, there is a well-regarded hospital close by this village at Tyndal Priory. Let me tell them of your wife's need, and they will send someone for her. I know your…"

"Forgive me if I offend, but my child must not be born on priory grounds. Babes of my people are often baptized against the will of the parents. The child is then placed in a Christian family because he may no longer live with his Jewish parents, unless they also convert. Perhaps you can understand why one of my faith would be wary."

Suddenly, Ralf grew angry. "You would cling to your faith and let your wife die?"

Jacob paled but said nothing for a moment, then asked, "Are you married, my lord?"

"Your question is impertinent. What is your point?"

"If you and your pregnant wife were stranded in the land ruled by those you deem heretics, would you foreswear your faith, deny the one whom you worship, if such were the price of saving her life?"

"A priest would say that your decision would not have the same weight as mine." Ralf responded as he believed proper for a Christian, but he secretly knew he would do anything to save Gytha's life were she the one bearing the child. He looked away, hoping to hide that weakness from ben Asser.

Jacob bowed. "If you have no further need to speak with me, I beg leave to attend my wife."

Ralf saw the redness in the man's brown eyes, deep lines in his forehead, and gray streaks in his black hair. If a man could age in a few moments of conversation, Jacob ben Asser had. Surely all these details had been present before, but the crowner had not noted them. "I have need to speak with you but not now. Go to your wife." He gestured at Cuthbert. "My sergeant will remain here as your guard. The other man…he has been detained."

Ben Asser murmured something and raced back inside.

Ralf spun around. "You will stay."

Cuthbert's eyes widened in horror. "Why? My wife…"

"She knows your duties for me often delay you."

"Let these people hire another to guard them."

Stepping closer to keep his words private, Ralf whispered: "No one in this village will do so. These are Jews. Their last guard has been murdered, and Mistress Signy overhead ben Asser arguing with him. Whatever the truth of the matter, he might be judged guilty of the crime simply because of his faith. If word spreads of this argument, the village may rise against the man and his frail wife, murdering both, before I can determine who should actually hang."

Cuthbert opened his mouth to protest further.

Ralf snarled.

The sergeant reluctantly agreed.

As the crowner turned away, he realized that Cuthbert held the same opinion of this family as his neighbors did. Who better to blame for the death of an unpopular man than Jacob ben Asser?

Chapter Nine

Gytha slipped behind the pewterer's stall and watched as Ralf left Cuthbert and went back inside the inn. If God were kind, the crowner would not have seen her.

"Are you ill, mistress?"

She shook her head and smiled at the youth, son of the master craftsman. He was a sweet lad with flaxen down on his cheeks. His brow, furrowed with concern, betrayed a kind heart as well as an ill-hidden attraction to the prioress' maid. "It is the sun," she replied. "I should have returned to the priory sooner."

He glanced around him, hoping to see the apprentice returning from the errand he had run. "I could carry that heavy basket for you on the road back."

"You are most considerate to suggest it, but your father needs you here for the customers." Gytha kept her tone both gentle and firm. "I shall not trouble you further."

He began to protest.

With a quick look toward the inn, she stepped away from the stall. "I am quite recovered," she said, knowing it would not be kind to torment the lad just because she could not face meeting the crowner.

As Gytha walked away, she knew she did not imagine the deep sigh coming from behind the display of finely crafted plate and vessels. Her own heart ached as well, but not for this merchant's son.

When the crowner had asked if he might walk with her through the stalls on this market day, she had given a grave assent even though her heart urged a more passionate reply. When had she not loved the man?

As a child, she had run circles around him, giggling with joy when he visited her brother. Later, when she reached marriageable age, she began teasing him with a flirtatious edge. At first, she was embarrassed by the change in her feelings but soon understood that he enjoyed her jests, even when he blushed. She learned to take pleasure in their brief moments of bantering. Although many men had wanted her as wife, begging Tostig for permission, he had honored her refusals. Only Ralf the Crowner filled her with both comfort and excitement.

Yet he had never approached Tostig with a proposal even though she was quite convinced the failure was not from lack of interest. She knew of his past love for Sister Anne. The one marriage to a woman of rank and property was expected, and she had accepted it. Despite her youth, Gytha had always owned a clear eye, but now matters were different. He was a widower with a daughter she adored.

His growing shyness, when she came to see his child, and the boyish color on his cheeks, when he asked to carry her basket on market day, proved he certainly liked her enough to bed. But he would never disgrace her or her brother by seeding a bastard in her so casually. For all his flaws, and she loved him in spite of many, Ralf owned an honorable heart.

So why had he not asked her to be his next wife? His rank might be above hers, but everyone in the village knew he had no love for a courtier's life and had heard how he refused to marry another of Sir Fulke's choosing. When he asked to accompany her this day, she did wonder if it was the time he might finally inquire if she were willing to share his life.

She felt tears sting her eyes. Then she had hoped for happiness. Now she felt only sorrow. How much had changed in such a short time.

"Mistress Gytha!"

Quickly rubbing the moisture from her cheeks, she turned to see the spice seller waving. His broad grin was a welcome distraction. Smiling in return, Gytha hurried to his stall.

"I have something special for Sister Matilda's kitchen and mayhap for your hospital as well," he said and turned to dig around in a large wooden box behind him.

Taking in a deep breath, she savored the mixed scents of sharp and sweet. Only the Master of Creation could create such wondrous plants with so many uses: dying cloth, curing disease, and flavoring food. Everything had a purpose, even if it had yet to be discovered. God wasted nothing, or so she was convinced.

And this merchant bought his treasures from lands so distant that they seemed mythical. He had many tales to tell of the origins of his wares, and Gytha was always eager to hear them, even if she did not really believe there were two-headed men or those with faces in their stomachs.

The extra time she spent with the spice merchant was hardly idle amusement. Prioress Eleanor required her charges to obey the rule banning red meat but encouraged Sister Matilda to exercise her cooking magic with vegetables, fruit, and fish. What Gytha brought back from market days delighted the nun in charge of the kitchen as well as the religious. Obedience to the rule did not mean denial of all culinary pleasure, and Gytha was happy to contribute to that joy.

She leaned forward. What did he have to show her now? Gytha almost forgot her sadness as she waited to see what the man would pull from the divided box.

Having found what he wanted, the spice merchant returned to the stall front and carefully opened his hand. His smile was as bright as that of a boy offering his mother a colorful flower. "This is saffron," he said in a voice soft with wonder.

Gytha looked closer at the reddish-gold threads resting in his palm.

"A miracle of God's creation," he said, "just arrived from a land beyond Outremer. The man who sold it to me said that it was prized by Moses when he lived in Pharaoh's court. Wise physicians claim it heals wounds, cures confused thoughts, and counters black bile."

"A miracle indeed if it does all that," she replied, but her jest was lightly spoken. Had she not dealt with this merchant long enough to know his honesty, she would have mocked him for thinking her so easily deceived and walked away.

As if reading her mind, he grinned. "All that might interest Sister Anne, but Sister Matilda would enjoy the flavor it adds to her cooking. And I can attest to its value in food, for I have eaten a fish stew with saffron added."

Would it please Ralf? Gytha felt her face turn hot. "Fish? Indeed!" She bent quickly over his hand again to hide her blush.

"I cannot describe the flavor, but I closed my eyes and wondered if the fish was still swimming in the sea. It is like nothing else I have tasted. And all it requires is a pinch of these threads, left for a day in wine, to add to a soup."

"And what is the price of this wonder?"

The merchant quickly looked around, and then bent to pick up a small jar that was meant to hold the more fragile spices. "It must be kept dry or it loses its power," he said, dropping the amount held in his hand into the container and sealing it shut. "Speak of no one about this, Mistress Gytha, for the item is costly, but I gift this small sample to the priory for the good of my soul."

She carefully nestled the jar into her basket. "As our prioress has said, the gift given unobserved shines more brightly in God's eyes than one presented with trumpet and cymbals." She gave him a studied look. "And only she shall know of your generosity. But our lady will not let a good man suffer for his charity and shall order more from you if it delights as you have suggested and our funds permit. Please whisper the cost in my ear."

He bent over and mumbled a figure.

Gytha swallowed a gasp but willed herself to nod with solemn dignity.

Thanking the merchant again for his gift, and promising to return the container the following week, she checked to make sure the item was safely balanced. Without looking up, she stepped away from the stall.

"Watch where you are going!"

Gytha stumbled backward.

Adelard stood in front of her. The sun glinting off his silver cross was as harsh as the look in his eyes. "Did you not see me walk toward you? It is your place to step aside, daughter of Eve."

"Surely it is a small courtesy to travel along one side of the crowd rather than down the middle where others, burdened as I am with a market basket, must squeeze against the stalls."

"I was praying. All should stand aside when they meet a man who is humbly communing with God." He folded his arms.

I have seen roosters crow at the sun with more humility, she noted silently, then replied: "I fear you have forgotten the Lord's teaching, for your tone lacks the modesty of which you speak, Adelard." She put her free hand on one hip. "I may be God's lesser creation, being Eve's daughter, but Adam's sons are most in danger of unacknowledged pride."

"How dare you preach to me?" His face burned with anger. "Saint Paul ordered all women to be silent and obedient, and so your words are a grave and profane sin."

Gytha gazed upward and tried not to beg God to strike this annoying youth speechless for the term of his earthly life. When she returned to the priory, she would have to ask if this noxious being had truly requested entrance to Tyndal as a novice. Was there ever gold enough to warrant taking such an arrogant man into a place set aside for peace and brotherhood?

"Step away." He waved at her.

Looking over her shoulder at the inn, Gytha decided that she dare not delay further and chance a meeting with the crowner. Even if she preferred flinging barbed retorts at the baker's son, a battle she most probably would win, this was one time she knew she should retreat with feigned submissiveness. She'd humble him another day.

Gytha stepped to one side.

"Whore," he muttered as he passed her by. "Did I not see you coupling with a liegeman of the Evil One in Satan's darkness below Ivetta the Whore's cottage?"

As if exposed to a sudden ice storm, her heart froze. Then fire flowed through her arms and legs as if the Devil himself had set a torch to her.

Just a few stalls down, Oseberne suddenly appeared and bellowed for his son to come help with the customers.

Adelard hissed something incomprehensible and ran to meet his father.

With as much self-control as she could muster, Gytha walked slowly away from the stalls and bustle of the crowds. Once she reached the edge of the village, she began to run, fleeing toward the priory like a deer escaping the hunter.

When she finally reached a quiet spot near the hut of Ivetta the Whore, a place cleansed of sin after Brother Thomas lived there as a hermit, she slipped into the brush to escape all eyes, sank to her knees, and wept.

Chapter Ten

Brother Gwydo finished binding the end of the straw coil with which he planned to construct a new skep for his bees. Setting it down beside him with the other coils, he watched the creatures flying to and from the previous huts he had made for them. One skep seemed especially busy, and the entrance must be cut larger to allow easier access. When the time came to weigh the skeps in the autumn, he was certain that one would be heavy enough with honey to allow the bees to survive the bitter cold of winter.

He sighed. Although he must kill the bees in the lighter skeps, harvesting the honey that was insufficient for them to feed upon until the weather warmed, he hated applying the deadly sulphur smoke. Bees were peaceful things. They reminded him of monks with their diligence, shared community, and utter devotion to the king. Killing them seemed cruel, almost unnatural. In biblical times, men took the honey and left the bees alone. Perhaps he could invent a way of returning to that less destructive time, harvesting honey and yet allowing these wonderful creations of God to survive.

Then there was the problem of the two skeps nearest the path to the mill where the bees remained hostile. Boys had thrown pebbles at them, knocking one skep off its platform. After chasing the lads away, he returned to right the hive and had been stung several times for his efforts. The attack had been warranted, he quickly forgave the bees, but the creatures still assaulted any who came too close.

And what had possessed those lads to molest beasts that had done them no harm? Men may have been made in God's image, but mortals seemed to take on the Devil's nature when it came to pointless aggression.

Shivering, Gwydo leaned his head back against the bark of the tree. He, too, had been like those boys once, although none would have questioned the virtue of his intent. When the bishop came to preach the crusade, he had taken the oath, rushing off to save Jerusalem from the infidel, mocking all who failed to heed the plea, and cursing any who were not Christian.

But then he saw soldier pilgrims rape girls, mere children, when they crawled for refuge into the dead arms of their mothers, and men take delight in torturing captives who had even sworn to accept baptism. It was then he asked how God could forgive such brutal acts, many against fellow Christians.

In those days, blood's stench filled his nostrils even in sleep, and one day he, too, shook hands with Death on the battlefield but survived. His own sins might have been lesser ones, but he came to believe that he was branded with the mark of Cain. Had he not been taught that all men were brothers? And he had slaughtered many of them.

When he confessed these musings to his priest and questioned the justice of killing even unbelievers, the man had gasped in horror, proclaiming that Satan had blinded him if he doubted that God delighted in the massacre of the infidel. And so Gwydo had ceased telling anyone of his qualms and decided to turn his back on the world. But he still wondered whether God or the Devil had whispered in his ear and condemned the bloodshed.

Closing his eyes and listening to the soothing hum of the bees in his care, he decided the answer might not matter. At Tyndal Priory, he had found tranquility in prayer and service. Here he had shed both rank and kin. His wife and his aged father believed he had died of a fever in Acre. His father had other sons. His wife could remarry, believing herself to be a widow. Some might say that was a sin, but other wives had done so in ignorance and

God surely forgave women, creatures rarely possessed of reason, more easily than He did the sons of Adam.

And so now he spent his remaining days laboring in the fields, praying for forgiveness, and tending bees with little enough harm done as the price of his peace. Only one last thing troubled his soul, one he dared not confess to any priest, a sin from his past that must somehow be expiated.

He had not believed it to be important until he overheard tales about Kenelm. Then he had awakened one night with a voice in his ear, telling him what he must do. A priest would have said it was the Devil, but, like his belief that he had wrongly slain his fellow men, Gwydo feared most it was God. And thus he had obeyed Him.

Perhaps he could have asked Brother Thomas about his plight, for this was a man not only of great virtue, but with much experience of Man's dual nature of good and evil. Might he not treat his concerns with compassion? Yet he hesitated. Would the good monk turn from him in horror as his former priest had done? He was not sure he could bear rejection from one whom he so admired.

Squeezing his eyes shut, Gwydo forced himself to ban the roar of terror and listen only to the calming music created by God's earthly miracles: clicking insects, rustling leaves dancing in the soft breeze, and the distant hiss of the sea. Once again, he slipped into sweet tranquility and left behind the burning wound of his mortal flaws. Surely God did not condemn him, for He had mercifully led him to this holy place. Satan was devious, but the Prince of Darkness never sent his minions to kneel before God's altar, find joy in service to the needy, and to toil in the cleansing of their souls.

Sighing, he turned his head and looked through the brushwood toward the mill pond. For a moment, his eyes grew heavy and he almost fell asleep.

But from just beyond the mill a woman appeared, walking slowly down the path toward him. Her head was bowed, and her pace suggested little eagerness to reach her destination.

Sliding into a sitting position against the tree, he recognized Gytha. She had been visiting the market day stalls, he concluded, seeing her full basket. Sister Matilda would be eager for whatever the maid had found for her. Indeed, the simple meals at Tyndal Priory gave him far greater delight than anything he had eaten at his father's more sumptuous table.

The maid stopped near where Gwydo sat under his tree. She quickly ran the edge of her hand under her eyes and down both cheeks. Was she weeping?

His heart began to pound with both sympathy and fear. Although he sometimes spoke with the worthy virgins vowed to God's service, he never did so alone. To be in the company of one who had never sworn herself to holy chastity made him tremble.

Gwydo squirmed under the bush on his belly. The maid must not see him. But he still had a full view of the path. Looking to his right toward the priory church, he saw Brother Thomas approaching.

The monk stopped. "Are you well?" he asked the young woman, his voice deep with concern.

"A bit of dust got in my eye." Gytha smiled with stiff brightness.

Now Brother Gwydo feared most that the pair would discover his presence and accuse him of deliberately listening in secret. Embarrassed, he pulled himself deeper into the brushwood.

Thomas did not pursue his suspicion that the maid had been crying. Instead, he pointed to the basket on the young woman's arm. "And what did you bring to delight Sister Matilda?" He grinned with the happier change of subject.

"Have you heard of saffron?" Gytha sounded relieved.

"Shall you give me a hint? Is it beast or herb?"

"A miracle of healing which also brings delight to the tongue, if the spice merchant is to be believed."

He peered into the basket. "Since I do not see it, I fear that Solomon's sword will be too large to divide the marvelous thing between kitchen and hospital."

Gytha pulled out the small jar and let him look. "It is the color of your hair, Brother." She looked up at him and smiled with evident affection. "If the merchant had not sworn this was edible, I might have believed someone stole a pinch from your head when it was last shaven."

Thomas rubbed the dense auburn thatch around his tonsure. "Most would say this was my curse," he replied softly.

"Are you going into the village?" Gytha carefully tucked the precious spice back into her basket.

"Prioress Eleanor wants me to question young Adelard about his longing to become a novice here."

A shadow clearly passed over her face.

Gwydo found that curious.

"Perhaps I shall also discover something useful regarding the murder." Staring over her shoulder at the gate leading to the village, he asked, "Did you hear anything in the market about Kenelm's death? Have men begun to discuss the crime?"

She visibly shivered. "As I was passing by the baker's stall, two women were talking and wondered if the Jewish family had something to do with it. They had heard that Kenelm was murdered on priory grounds."

"The word has spread quickly." Thomas looked unhappy. "Someone must have seen us searching above the mill wheel near the gate."

"Then you did find evidence he was killed here?" She raised a hand to her mouth. "Not on the road…or above the village, as our crowner thought?"

Thomas nodded. "So it would appear. There is still a chance that he was grievously wounded outside the priory but crawled through the gate to seek help from…. Mistress Gytha!"

As she started to fall, Thomas instinctively grasped her around the waist. It took only a moment for her to recover, then her eyes opened and she blinked at the man in whose arms she rested.

"The sun, Brother," she said. "It is only that. I fear the heat today has disturbed my humors." She tapped his arm.

He released her and stepped back.

Gwydo began to shake as if he suffered an ague, and his teeth chattered. Fearing the pair could hear the sound, he jammed his fingers into his mouth.

But the couple said little more. Gytha declined the monk's offer of assistance back to the prioress' chambers.

Thomas' brow was furrowed with worry, but he bowed silent acceptance of her refusal and walked on toward the gate leading to the village.

The maid hurried off, stopping once to look over her shoulder before disappearing into the nuns' quarters.

Gwydo pulled himself out of his hiding place and stood up, stretching his stiff back. His heart was heavy. Although neither maid nor monk had committed a grave wrongdoing, the lay brother was deeply troubled. Thomas should never have embraced her as he did. Was the gesture an innocent error or had it signified something unchaste between them?

Had he been wrong about the monk's virtue? As for Gytha, she was a woman, a temptress like all of her sex. Just one touch, even one suffered in a compassionate act, and a man's chastity was endangered. He knew how he weakened in his resolve. But perhaps Brother Thomas was as strong in his faith as Robert of Arbrissel, founder of this Order who went into bordels to preach? Once again, Gwydo doubted his ability to differentiate between virtue and sin.

"Most certainly I erred in pointing out that this murder may have occurred here. It was wicked pride that made me do it. I wanted Brother Thomas to look with favor on me for discovering something no one else had."

Deep in thought, Gwydo walked back to where he had left his coils of woven straw and bent to pick them up. Suddenly, he turned pale, straightened, and shook his fists at the heavens. "Wherever you may be, Satan," he roared, "I curse you for blinding me so I could not see the consequences of my heinous deed!"

What was he to do? He struck his head and groaned. "I must, I shall make amends for my sins." In frustration, he squeezed his eyes shut and moaned.

He could do nothing now. The road outside the priory would be filled with men, wearied from many hours of labor and traveling back to their homes in the village. Taking a deep breath, he tried to calm himself. Later he could hunt for something that would convince Crowner Ralf and Prioress Eleanor that the murder had actually happened outside the priory walls. He would apologize for his error in believing he had discovered evidence to prove otherwise, an arrogance for which he would welcome any penance.

But he must find a way to leave the priory while it was still light enough to hunt for what he might use to do this. How to explain this new discovery to the prioress was a problem he would cope with later. After all, he had no right to leave these grounds without her permission. He must expect severe punishment for this act alone.

Compared to the sins he had already committed, he decided that was the least of his transgressions.

Chapter Eleven

The air was cool after the late night rain. Birds rejoiced as the moist soil yielded fat worms. Plants glistened, stretched forth their leaves and welcomed the morning sun.

Chapter had ended, and the nuns left the chamber in an orderly fashion to attend their various tasks. They were silent, arms folded into their sleeves and heads bowed. For most, prayer was their primary duty in this life they had chosen, and they longed to return to it.

Prioress Eleanor, however, was restless. Although the reports on wool profits and incoming rents needed attention, she feared she could not concentrate on them. Instead, she went back to her private quarters, knelt at her prie-dieu and sought the relief found in more prayer.

The worldly businesses of the priory might not have kept her mind tethered to the earth, but other matters most certainly did.

With a courteous apology to God, she leapt up and hurried back down the stone steps to the cloister garth. Her favored cat, named after the King Arthur of legend and dreams, trotted after with a noticeable joy in his gait.

As she entered the garden, Eleanor let herself be lost in the profuse growth that hid walls and only allowed an open view of the sky above. This was a peaceful place, one where all the nuns went from time to time to find the silence needed to rediscover God, for noise and human pain were still found in cloistered worlds. In gardens, even the wind was hushed.

Arthur, the orange tabby, sprinted ahead of her and began to investigate what might lie hidden under the moist leaves. Eleanor smiled at him with love, then briefly closed her eyes and took a deep breath.

This garth was tended by Sister Edith, a nun whose touch was so skilled that many believed God had shared some of His secrets from the creation of Eden with her. When winter brought bitter cold, life here never quite ended. There remained a sense that all was simply asleep until the spring. Some said the garth reminded them of the promise of resurrection. All found balm for wounded souls.

Only here did Eleanor find that absolute stillness which allowed God to whisper in her ear. The chapel might be a setting for contemplation but bustling creatures, praying mortals, and the stones themselves produced intrusive sounds. In this place, nature took a submissive role, demanding no notice and offering only a gentle comfort. She glanced down. Even in heat of the day, flowers were soft and fragrant; the purple star-shaped ones with yellow centers were among her favorites.

As she turned to look at the murmuring fountain, however, she recalled that even this sanctuary had once been blighted with murder. Only days after her arrival years ago, Sister Anne had found a corpse here. Eleanor's memory of Brother Rupert's cruelly mutilated body was as vivid as if he still lay just in front of her.

She sat on a stone bench and began to feel a slight throbbing over her left eye. Pressing her fingers against the spot, she prayed that God would be merciful and not let one of her severe headaches strike now of all times. Although the feverfew she took at Sister Anne's suggestion eased much of the pain, she had begun to suffer more from flashing lights, shimmering colors, and other strange sights as a forewarning of the headaches.

She stared back at the purple flower. There was no glittering halo of light surrounding it. The mild throbbing began to recede. God had been kind.

She must think clearly about Kenelm's slaying. Stiffening both back and will, she drove the panic she felt over this new murder on priory grounds into exile. Just because violence had invaded Tyndal again did not mean one of her religious was guilty of the crime.

It would not be the first time she had had to consider the possibility. Each time she prayed it would be the last. Now her stomach roiled with fury that the question must even be addressed. She looked up and silently asked God why He chose to vex her so over and over. Surely the death of Brother Rupert several years ago had not been meant as a sign.

Eleanor stared upward as she fought to quiet her soul's complaint. It was not for her to demand. It was her duty to serve God without question. "If my function on this earth is to war against those who commit the ultimate crime, so be it," she conceded, but she still did so with teeth clenched.

The clouds, like tangles of sheep wool, scuttled across the blue sky. Overhead, a dark-headed hawk flew by. Its flight was leisurely, seemingly without purpose, but such languor belied its deadly mission. In the open grounds of Tyndal Priory, an unlucky rodent would soon be dinner.

And so Death hovers over us all, she mused. We can only pray it comes as a good death and not against God's plan.

She rubbed the palm of her hand on the stone and felt jagged spots, although the bench was well-crafted. There was an allegory in that, she decided. Tyndal was dedicated to purity of thought and deed, but sharp-toothed serpents lived within the walls. No one wished to hear that anyone sworn to God's service could commit a heinous crime, but she had seen too much of Man's darker side to ever ignore the possibility.

"But who could it be this time?" she murmured and ran through a list of all who dwelt here. The nuns were sequestered with a few exceptions. Her sub-prioress dealt with the world, but she was no killer despite her querulous nature. Sister Anne and Sister Christina oversaw the care given at the hospital. The former was a healer, and the latter utterly incapable of violence. Almost all the women, lay sisters included, had been here when she came to lead them. Anchoress Juliana was the exception, but

Eleanor had cause to know that she had faithfully remained in her enclosure.

As for the monks, they were few in number and, again, most had been in residence long before she arrived. Brother Thomas was more recent, but he had entered Tyndal shortly after she did.

She had already spoken with Prior Andrew about those under his authority, both lay and choir brothers. After that trouble when Father Eliduc visited two summers ago, she was confident Andrew had thoroughly investigated the possibility that a monk might have killed Kenelm. According to the prior, no one knew this man who had come so recently to the village. Gossip always breached priory walls, but only one monk admitted he had heard the dead man's name.

That left the lay brothers, who labored in the fields or hospital so the choir monks might spend a greater portion of their hours on their knees. Beseeching God to save the souls of His flawed creation kept the latter too busy to harvest or tend coughs. Many courtiers had paid for this mercy, with land or other wealth given to the priory. There were many lay brothers at Tyndal as a consequence.

Last evening, Andrew had questioned the eldest and most reliable of the lay brothers. Although Brother Beorn was quarrelsome and judgmental, the man struggled to be fair, humbly prefacing his remarks with a warning that he suffered many imperfections. After uttering complaints about the laziness of one lay brother and the garrulousness of another, Brother Beorn finally mentioned Brother Gwydo, the newest member at the priory. Prior Andrew told his prioress that Beorn was uncharacteristically reluctant to speak ill of the man, yet he had expressed some unease.

Both she and Prior Andrew had approved Gwydo's plea to remain here for the rest of his days. Having been a soldier, Andrew especially understood the need for a man to leave a warrior's life, no matter how noble the cause of war. Eleanor's eldest brother had joined King Edward on crusade, and she had seen the change wrought in her once joyful sibling. The decision to admit Gwydo was an easy one.

When she asked the cause of Beorn's discomfort, Andrew had shaken his head and confirmed that the elder lay brother could not explain it. "I have often thought Brother Gwydo to be of higher birth than he has claimed," the prior said. "Once he responded when Brother Thomas used a Latin phrase as if he knew the language. That suggests more education than a common soldier might own."

"Or else his parish priest taught him, hoping the bright lad might find a calling with the Church," Eleanor had replied.

Perhaps they should have questioned Gwydo more about his past, she wondered, but he had come to their hospital to die, his eventual survival counting as one of the many miracles here.

Now sitting in the garth and watching a bumblebee roll inside a bright pink flower, she could think of no good reason to suspect a man of murder because he might know a little Latin or be a soldier of undisclosed rank. A desire for humble service should be cause for celebration, not suspicion, especially if the supplicant was of high rank. A rare event perhaps, but there were examples to be found amongst the saints.

Watching the bee fly away, she rose and began to stroll along the gravel pathways of the garth, keeping her thoughts still. Here and there, Eleanor paused to smell a sweet scent or wonder at the delicate beauty of the local wildflowers Sister Edith chose to intermingle with other flowers deemed nobler.

She glanced behind her.

Her cat followed, now accompanied by a brown-striped female of his ilk.

Eleanor chuckled. Her beloved Arthur had shown extraordinary devotion to this particular cat, who served to keep the hospital free of offending rodents. This pair must have produced enough kittens over the last six years to rid all East Anglia of mice and rats.

Had she truly been prioress that long? Naïve as she may have been when first appointed to the position by King Henry III, she had lost much innocence since her twentieth year. Although Brother Gwydo did not trouble her for the same reasons he did

Brother Beorn, she could not assume he was completely innocent of any wrong. Since he was the newest member of the priory, and the one whose past was least well known, she must seek more information about the man. If there was anything pertinent found, she would consider the details with an uncompromising impartiality. Any error made in approving his entrance would be hers, a mistake she'd openly confess.

Hearing the bells ring for the next office, she was thankful. Her prayers would include a plea that God grant her that clear and just mind she needed. In this, He had rarely failed her.

And soon she would meet with Crowner Ralf, show him the latest findings, and pose her questions. In truth, what troubled her most was not that one of her religious might have sinned but that the crime had been committed on priory land. There was no doubt in her mind that there was a reason for that.

Might the killer have such an extreme quarrel with Tyndal that he would ignore God's wrath to shed blood here? That conclusion seemed unlikely, yet… She willed herself not to think further on that.

Taking one last deep breath of the summer air, Prioress Eleanor turned into the path that led to the chapel.

As she drew closer to God's house, she felt lighter in spirit. Surely she had done all she could, given what she knew of Kenelm's death. Sending Brother Thomas to visit the baker, Oseberne, and his son, Adelard, was a good decision. Of course her monk's opinion on the suitability of the young man as a novice was crucial, but she also knew Thomas would take time to learn more about the dead man as she had suggested. Whether gossip or fact, something must cast light on why this slaying had been done and why in Tyndal. She should not worry about possibilities without cause.

Just before she left the garth, she heard a noise and looked over her shoulder. Her cat and his lady were just slipping into the greenery, those loud meows suggestive of amorous intent.

More kittens to terrify mice and serve God? Amused, she laughed quietly but suspected He might share her mirth.

Chapter Twelve

Standing behind his kneeling son, Oseberne stared without blinking at the monk and waited.

Adelard's eyes glowed with rampant hope.

Thomas bowed his head to gain some time before continuing this difficult interview. Someone else ought to have been sent here. Of all people, he had no right to render judgment on any suppliant novice. Never had he had a true calling and, considering his ongoing quarrel with God, his own faith was questionable.

Taking a deep breath, he avoided the father's sharp gaze and turned his attention back to the youth. Looking upon him with feigned gravity, Thomas prayed he appeared sufficiently pious.

The baker cleared his throat with undisguised impatience.

Thomas fought against his dislike of Adelard. After his experience two summers ago, he had become uncomfortable around those who were too eager to convince others of their devotion to God. He preferred the faithful who quietly served with simple compassion, like Sister Anne and Sister Christina. The baker's son crowed for attention.

"I see so much evil in the world, Brother," Adelard was saying, his eyes squeezed shut and his prayerful hands clenched so fiercely that the outline of the knuckles shone through the flesh.

The father grunted approvingly, his red jowls trembling with fervor. Beside him stood his youngest son, a spotty-faced child approaching the cusp of manhood whose body stank more than most. The lad scratched at a round, scaly patch near his ear, and a drop of blood began to weave down his neck.

"The final days of this wicked earth must be nigh. I expect soon to hear the trumpets declaring the End."

Although Thomas had no doubt that the world must end as the gospels proclaimed, he often wondered if the last day might come, not with the expected roaring but rather a preternatural silence. Man had always been so boisterous with wickedness that a sudden quietness might be more terrifying than the clashing of swords and belching of fire-spitting dragons. He blinked, realizing he had not responded. "Why do you say so, my son?"

"Do not the Jews roam freely amongst good Christian men?"

An odd remark, especially after the king had just restricted all Jewish families to living in the small number of *archa* towns. That seemed more a constraint on movement than any increased freedom. Thomas did not try to hide his confusion. It was, after all, his purpose here to query, not to teach. "Explain that statement more fully."

Adelard seemed at a loss to reply and looked over his shoulder at his father.

"What need is there to say more?" The baker stiffened. "I, myself, have seen the horns on their heads and smelled the Devil's fetid smoke exuding from them. Their presence contaminated Tyndal village over the winter and early spring, and now their malignant influence befouls us again with the arrival of this current family. Surely your priory has felt their evil clawing at your own stone walls."

Thomas wrinkled his nose. The only odor he noticed came from the baker's youngest son. No matter what Oseberne and his eldest son believed, Thomas most certainly had never seen horns or smelled Satan's breath in his contacts with the king's people.

As a matter of fact, Thomas agreed with those Church leaders who urged patience over the slow conversion of the Jews to Christianity. Did Saint Paul not say in his letter to the Romans that all Gentiles must first be converted and then Israel? As far as the monk knew, there were many more people left in that former category.

Adelard nodded with enthusiasm. "The Jews have overwhelmed our land!" His gaze grew distant and his face turned bright with passion. Although he lacked his father's jowls, his face matched the paternal color well.

"The roads have been filled with the creatures," Oseberne added. "I fear for the safety of the children in this village! Remember how our sainted William was crucified by them in Norwich!" Sweat glistened in the furrows that crossed his brow, and he nodded pointedly at his youngest son.

Bored, the boy had begun to rock from side to side.

"And since no child here has suffered injury, Master Baker, your fears are for naught." As far as Thomas was concerned, this exodus was no apocalyptical sign but the result solely of a secular, political decision. "After our king and his mother ordered the Jews to leave Cambridge, most came through here on the way to Norwich. They stayed no longer than one night before departing. The village gained in coin. The priory suffered no harm."

"We had children die of fever last winter," Oseberne snapped.

"We grieve for all parents who suffered a child's death, but Sister Anne says fewer died here than usual."

The baker stared at Thomas' feet, as if confirming that he lacked cloven hooves, then shook his head.

"Was not Kenelm slaughtered on priory ground?" Adelard raised a finger heavenward. "And we have a Jewish family here now. Surely these facts together have meaning."

Thomas felt his earlier unease grow even greater. How swiftly that detail of Kenelm's death had spread.

Oseberne dropped a hand heavily on his eldest son's shoulder. "If they cannot pollute wells, they will be driven to find some other way to profane our holy ground."

"How did you learn that tale?" Thomas frowned.

"My son heard some women talking about it after they left my stall." The baker squeezed his fingers around Adelard's collar bone. "My special loaves are popular with many."

The lad winced, then nodded.

Thomas felt a shiver of fear. These accusations of sacrilege, voiced by the baker, were becoming more common. The safer days of Henry II's reign, a king who did not tolerate harassment of the Jewish community, were long past. This current king was pulling back both his favor and protection.

As for these tales of fouling water, crucifying children, or drinking Christian blood, he knew they were slanders born of hate, and the stories were often used to explain unsolved murders and other violence. In this matter of Kenelm's death, the myths suited those fearful of an unknown killer and longing to turn the accusing finger away from a village man and toward a much preferred scapegoat.

The youngest son began to tug on his father's sleeve.

Oseberne growled at him.

Grimacing, the child cupped his hand between his legs.

Thomas hoped the baker would let the boy go relieve himself elsewhere.

Oseberne grunted and waved his hand.

The youngster fled.

"Are you suggesting these travelers killed their own guard?" Thomas now welcomed the shift in discussion. He was straying from his obligation to dig deeper into Adelard's longing for priory life, but Prioress Eleanor had also hoped he might gather useful information about the killing.

Adelard looked amazed, as if the question lacked all reason. "Kenelm was undoubtedly full of sin, but wasn't he still a Christian? They hate us as the Devil tells them they should. Of course they killed him!"

Even if the family housed in Signy's stable did hate Christians, Thomas thought, they would have been preternaturally stupid if they killed the one person hired to protect them. The Jewish men he had met in his clerical days had been neither better nor worse than those of Christian faith and certainly possessed the same measure of wits.

Oseberne and Adelard gazed at the monk, eagerly anticipating his reply.

"An odd thing to do, however. Surely they have heard how others of their faith suffered theft and harassment despite the king's plea that they be allowed to travel in safety. Without Kenelm, they lacked any shield against violence."

Straightening his back, Adelard proved to be his father's true son as he released a fulsome snort. "Knowing these people to be the Devil's spawn, I watched them. Not long before his body was found, Kenelm mocked the Jew's faith. Surely he was killed for the truth of his words."

Once again the father's hand clutched Adelard's shoulder and squeezed it. "My son heard the man called Jacob argue with the dead man. They scuffled." Oseberne looked down at his son who tilted his head back to stare up at his father. "Did you not overhear the Jew threaten to kill his Christian guard?"

Adelard looked back at the monk and nodded with enthusiasm.

"It is not surprising that Kenelm was found dead in the priory mill pond. Is that not a sacrilege?" The baker hesitated, and then his scowl fled to be replaced with a delighted smile. "And a deliberate contamination of your water! The stream is like your well, is it not?"

Thomas shuddered. His qualms regarding what these rumors might bring were coming to fruition.

"Now you see, Brother, how these wicked people have committed violence against us." Adelard lifted his silver cross and kissed it.

"I shall report your words to our crowner," the monk said. "He may wish to question you." And he would alert his prioress as well. He could only hope that Adelard had not already spread this story amongst the villagers but suspected the damage had already been done.

Oseberne was looking at his son's cross with pride. "I gave him that," he said to the monk.

Does this man care only about his fine loaves and being perceived as a man able to buy a silver cross? Thomas was annoyed but knew he must now pull himself back from inquiring into Kenelm's death and return to the stated purpose of his visit here.

Glancing down at the youth, he saw a shadow pass over Adelard's face as he contemplated that silver cross of which his father boasted. Then the monk looked back at the baker standing behind his son. The man was imposing in size, his son frail by comparison. It was easy to see how such an intimidating father could impose his will on the young man.

It was an observation worth pursuing. Just how much of the youth's proclaimed passion for the cloister came from Oseberne and how much desire for the religious life arose from Adelard's own heart? If this youth's calling was sincere, the monk hoped it had a gentler side that could be cultivated. That rough-edged fanaticism made Adelard sound like a younger version of his father. In Thomas' opinion, hate might be better applied to pounding bread dough than taking on a monk's life.

"Whatever the resolution of this murder, the presence of Jews in Tyndal shall be temporary, but, if you are accepted as a novice at Tyndal priory, that shall last a lifetime. Surely you have reasons for longing to abandon the world other than a hatred of the Jews."

"Women! I can no longer bear their presence. By day, they play the honest virgin. At night, they whore. My dreams are so rife with succubae that I cannot sleep and instead war against the darkness with the sharp sword of prayer."

Recalling his own dismay at the same age when a light touch on his groin might transform him into a leering satyr, he suspected Adelard suffered a similar shame and fear. "Satan often sends his imps to torment men at night." His voice was gentle with understanding.

"But the whores are not just in dreams! They walk the earth and lure good men into their foul embrace." He glanced back at his father. "Not all, of course. My mother was so chaste that she must be in Heaven now."

Thomas knew he had not imagined the baker's wince before the widower lowered his gaze and nodded.

"You have witnessed this evil yourself, my son?" The monk prepared to hear Adelard name every young woman in the village who might have shared a kiss with a youth.

Adelard's expression turned sly. "Lust infects many, Brother."

The monk froze as if the young man had caught him in some lewd act. Thomas quickly reminded himself that the subject was wanton women, a temptation to which he had long been immune. "You have proof?" he asked again.

"Mine own eyes."

"You witness much." Did this youth ever sleep? Of course, he often did not either, tormented as he was by his own particular longings.

"God has chosen me to point the finger of righteous outrage on His behalf, and thus I walk the paths during Satan's hours to seek out wickedness."

"Continue."

"I name Gytha, Tostig's sister, as our greatest harlot."

Thomas clenched his fist and drew back to keep from striking Adelard. If anyone was virtuous, it was Prioress Eleanor's maid, a woman beloved for both her kindness and ready wit. He felt his face turn hot with rage at the accusation.

Adelard read the flush of the monk's face differently. "I knew you would be horrified that your priory housed such a serpent." He glowed with pride at his revelation.

The monk nodded, not trusting himself to speak.

"There is more."

"Aye?" Thomas spat more than uttered his reply.

"She lay with Brother Gwydo near the hut of Ivetta the Whore. I witnessed the sin. That was the night of the murder."

Thomas' head spun and roaring filled his ears. Dizzy, he stepped back, braced his hand on the wall to steady himself, and willed away the bruising echo of Adelard's sordid accusation.

And so it took him a moment to understand that the deafening noise he heard was not caused by the passion of his outrage. Instead it was the shouting of an angry crowd in the street outside the baker's house.

Chapter Thirteen

Brother Thomas rushed into the road but was immediately shoved back against the house wall. The mob was so closely packed, it heaved like lice-infested hair.

Adelard and his father stayed safe within the doorway.

"Kill the Jews!" one man shouted. He elbowed his way past the monk and stabbed his pitchfork at the sky.

Thomas caught himself wondering why God must be pricked to pay attention. He tried to inch back to the protection of the baker's door.

A few feet in front of him, a man slipped in dung, lost his footing, and slid under trampling feet. Terrified and in pain, he began to scream.

The mob pushed on.

Thomas jammed his elbows into stomachs and backs until he reached the fallen man. The mass of people now slowed enough so he could drag the villager back to the doorway.

The baker and his son reluctantly made room.

Wide-eyed and whimpering, the injured victim clung to the monk's sleeve as if he might fall into Hell's pit should he let go.

"You are fortunate that these are minor wounds," Thomas said, examining a bloodied hand and facial cuts. "No broken bones. Go home to your good wife and let her use the healing herbs from the garden on those."

"But the Jews…"

"Do as I say unless you want the wounds to fester. Will any of your fellows here feed your family if that hand must be cut off?"

The man scrabbled to his feet, inched his way along the wall to the back of the milling throng, and sprinted down the road.

The crowd no longer moved, but their shouts grew shrill. Thomas covered his ears and stepped to one side of the door. As he did, he was roughly pushed back into the road.

It was Adelard who shoved him. The youth screamed, leaping from the doorway as the mob began to chant for blood. Raising his fists, he cried out for the slaughter of all who refused baptism. Then he bent his elbows, thrust his way deep into the roaring throng, and disappeared.

Despite the tumult, the monk heard a high-pitched scream behind him. He spun around, terrified that the mob had somehow invaded the baker's house.

But only Oseberne was inside. The man had clutched a handful of his youngest son's loose tunic to prevent him from following his older brother. The child's face was scarlet, tears pouring down his cheeks.

Thomas was unsure if the child howled out of terror or frustrated rage.

Without a word, the baker yanked the boy further into the house and slammed the door. The heavy wooden beam inside dropped with a thud and firmly sealed the door shut. The only path to safety from the riot now lay solely along a narrow space between the house wall and the crowd.

"Brother Thomas!"

That was Nute's voice! Frightened that the lad was injured, the monk stretched himself as high as he could to peer over the shouting men. Then he saw the boy, squeezed between two burly men.

Shouting that God would punish all who thwarted His will, Thomas pushed into the mob and fought his way toward the boy. This time, a small path opened as a few men edged aside, staring at the monk with trepidation. Rarely had they heard such anger from a religious, and never from this man whom they had good cause to respect.

Reaching the lad, he pulled Nute loose and hugged him close, then kicked shins and threatened hellfire until he got safely back to the baker's door.

"Are you hurt?" He fell to his knees and carefully checked Nute for broken ribs, foot, or arms.

The boy shook his head. Although he was pale with terror, he had not allowed himself to cry.

"You're a brave one," Thomas said, his voice warm with admiration for the courage of this child. Nonetheless, he kept Nute's hand firmly in his grasp.

"Why are they shouting so?" Nute crept as close to the monk as pride would allow.

Thomas just shook his head, failing to find any satisfactory way to explain how these men could use God to justify violence against another created in His image.

"They are headed for the stables." Nute pointed. "Mistress Signy must be warned!"

Again stretching onto his toes, Thomas peered over the tops of heads. Near the front of the crowd, Cuthbert was waving his arms. As the sea of men rose like a riptide around him, the sergeant's face took on the panicked look of a man about to drown. Not only was the Jewish family in danger of being ripped apart, but so was Ralf's bailiff and second-in-command. Thomas could delay action no longer.

The monk bent down and spoke into Nute's ear. "Can you find your way to the priory?" He rested one hand gently on the boy's thin shoulder.

Nute shivered. "Aye, Brother," he replied.

Thomas turned him around and pointed. "See that space along the wall? Ease your way through it, and you shall find yourself at the rear of this throng. Go, if you are willing. I'll watch until you break free."

Nute tightened his jaw and nodded. "I can do that."

"Run swiftly to the priory and tell the porter there is a riot in the village. Say that I have sent you to Prioress Eleanor. She told me that Crowner Ralf was meeting with her. He must return at once."

The lad repeated the message, pressed his back to the wall, and edged his way through the crowd. Thomas watched, then stood and peered toward the back of the chanting mob. With relief, he saw Nute emerge and race toward Tyndal Priory.

He would have preferred not to send the boy into danger, but he had no choice. This gathering of villagers was growing violent. The baker had taken his young son to safety and barricaded his door. Adelard had joined the mob. Cuthbert and the helpless family in the stables were trapped and in danger for their lives.

Praying that the crowner would come quickly, Thomas threw himself back into the mass of men waving tools and fists. Once again, he used sharp elbows and God's name to win his way through.

One man looked at the monk and squeezed against his neighbor to let Thomas pass. "Look!" He screamed, his round eyes devoid of all reason. "Brother Thomas is here. The priory blesses us for coming to slay the unbelievers!"

"Kill the Jews! Kill the Jews!" The chanting began again.

Grunting as he pushed himself closer to Cuthbert, Thomas prayed for strength. "Whatever my lacks," he murmured to God, "I beg for the gift bestowed on Moses, a voice that will save the innocent." Cuthbert had done nothing to deserve harm. Whether or not the man liked the duty, he was here on Ralf's orders. Even if this family, huddled in the stables, was involved in murder, they deserved a trial before being condemned.

Finally, Thomas reached the front of the mob. There he saw Adelard. The youth's eyes were glazed as if he had been granted some vision, but he stepped aside to let the monk through.

Cuthbert stood on the edge of a rough stone trough used to water horses. His eyes were red with weeping and he stank. His bowels had loosened.

Thomas tugged at the man's stained tunic to get his attention. "Step down," he said to the wide-eyed sergeant, "and go back toward the stable. The crowner is coming. I will talk to these men."

Cuthbert jumped down and fled.

Someone gave the monk a hand up, and the monk straddled the trough, balancing himself. "Why have you come here?" Thomas shouted.

"To kill the Jews!" several men shouted.

"Why?"

A stunned silence fell.

One standing next to the baker's son finally replied, his voice hoarse from yelling. "They have slain a Christian and polluted the priory water."

"They have murdered Kenelm and will crucify our Christian babes. They will drink their blood like wine for one of their feasts!" This from the man who had never stopped jabbing his pitchfork at God.

Several more shouted replies, but some of the nearby voices had grown oddly tentative.

Thomas raised his eyes and lifted his hands up to heaven as if he were listening to God's voice.

Most fell silent. Those who did not, lowered their speech to a mumbling.

Thomas let the moment of silence linger, then looked back at the crowd and dropped his arms into a gesture of embrace. "We do not know who killed Kenelm," he said. His deep voice was as gentle as his gaze.

The muttering grew louder.

"But Crowner Ralf shall find the one who did. When he does, the guilty will surely hang."

"None of us committed the crime, Brother. It must be the Jews. Who else would dare murder a man on holy ground, then drop the corpse into the mill pond?"

Thomas closed his eyes and again begged God to ignore all his faults and sins just this once. To quell the riot, he needed far more strength than any sinful mortal owned.

"Even if the Jews did not kill our townsman, they are a vile people whom God hates for killing His son." The man who spoke waved a thick cudgel.

A few cheers greeted those words.

"Dare you claim to be more learned in the faith than the saints?" Thomas raised his voice so all could hear, but his tone remained calm.

There was a hesitation, then a few scattered "nays." Perplexed, most grew still and stared at the monk.

"Or perhaps you think yourselves wiser than a pope who may speak on God's behalf?"

Even Adelard now shouted his denial of such blasphemy.

"Then hear this tale." Thomas stopped and waited until he was sure he had the crowd's complete attention. "Saint Bernard of Clairvaux himself once stood before a group of Christian men, like you, who had gathered to slaughter the Jews in their city. He condemned their intent and preached forbearance, for the holy Church has forbidden us to persecute or kill the Jews."

Such profound silence now prevailed that even the birds could be heard singing from the trees.

Adelard stared at the monk in disbelief. "Brother, this cannot be!"

Thomas was sweating but his voice remained strong. "For the sins these people have committed, they have been dispersed throughout all lands and made subject to the will of Christian rulers. In this land, our kings have put them under their protection from the days of the first William." He raised his hands for silence as some expressed outrage. "And King Edward, our liege lord and a man who wielded his sword in Outremer against all infidels, has done the same, knowing it is the will of the Church and in accordance with the expressed desire of Pope Gregory X."

Adelard's eyes lost their glitter. His shoulders slumped.

"As Saint Paul himself said, we may not slay the people of Israel. They shall, in good time, be saved when all the Gentiles have seen the truth of God's teaching. Were the Jews to be slaughtered, the final days could not come, the righteous never allowed their reward, nor the remaining penitent loosed from Purgatory by the coming of our Lord."

A few cried out in dismay, and two within the monk's view visibly shook. Thomas hoped he had instilled enough terror to douse their anger.

"Would you deny the souls of your loved ones the chance to be freed from torment sooner?" He swept his hand to encompass the entire village. "If you do not care for the pain they suffer, or for the agony you shall also know in time, then kill this family. If you fear God, lay down your weapons and return to your work as good Christians should do."

The baker's son reached up and touched the monk's robe. "If this be true, as you have said, there is much I do not understand, Brother." Tears began to slip down his cheeks, making streaks of white in the dust cast up in his face by so many feet. "I have never been told any of this."

"We are all imperfect and often ignorant, my son," the monk said directly to him. "It is only sinful to remain willfully blind to knowledge. Seeking truth and wisdom is never a transgression. As for the Jews, remember also this teaching. How can we do violence against those we call *enemy*? Are we not enjoined to love them?"

"Must we let these people live then?" The breath of the man who asked was foul.

"God demands it."

"And if they did kill a Christian?" The same man's eyes narrowed.

"The king's law shall rule on the killer's fate. Were you to proceed, as you intended, you would either commit treason by disregarding the king's will or you would be committing a graver sin by going against God's own commands. For the safety of your souls and your necks, I beg you to turn aside from this wicked purpose and return, in peace, to your homes."

The man with the pitchfork lowered it.

"Have faith that God's anointed king and our lord on earth shall seek justice for Kenelm's death. Indeed, Crowner Ralf is diligently pursuing the truth. As all of us know, he is a good man and a loyal subject of King Edward."

Thomas took a deep breath. Folding his arms into his sleeves, he tried to think of what more he could say to these men but failed to come up with any stronger arguments. Then he heard a commotion from the back of the crowd.

Ralf was approaching. Beside him walked several armed men, little Nute…and Oseberne?

Not believing what he saw, Thomas rubbed at his eyes.

The baker leaned over to say something to one of the men, then abruptly turned toward his own house.

How had Oseberne left without being seen?

Voices around him drew the monk's attention back to the throng. Although there was a low grumbling amongst them, they were dispersing. With gratitude, Thomas glanced upward and almost wept with relief. The oration and the crowner's timely arrival had worked.

Adelard, however, had not moved. His head remained bowed. With a groan, he now turned around and trudged slowly back to his father's house.

Perhaps the young man has learned something, Thomas thought as he watched the youth walk away. He ought to speak with the hopeful novice now, for this might be the time to uproot Adelard's irrational zeal and plant the seeds of a gentle compassion in him instead.

The monk jumped down from the trough.

A tug at his robe stopped him from following the baker's son.

Cuthbert knelt at the monk's feet. "Thank you, Brother. At the risk of your own, you saved my life!"

Thomas protested that he had done nothing so brave.

Grabbing the monk's robe, the man kissed the hem. "They were threatening to tear me to pieces, if I did not let them into the stables. They even swore they'd kill my family in front of me before they let me die!"

Thomas grasped the trembling sergeant, pulled him to his feet, and whispered soothing words in his ear. Out of the corner of his eye, he realized that the crowd had disappeared, leaving behind a haze of dust over the road.

Near the path to the stables, Ralf was speaking to a small group. The armed men, who had come with him, lounged against the wall of the inn but stepped aside to let Nute run in to seek Mistress Signy.

A few houses down, Oseberne greeted the distraught Adelard, grabbed him by the shoulder, and tried to pull him toward the house.

The young man shouted at his father, tore himself loose, and ran down the road toward the priory.

Thomas hesitated, then turned back to comfort Cuthbert.

The sergeant was no longer there.

Chapter Fourteen

The crowner slapped the monk's back. "I heard how you saved my sergeant and quelled the mob, Brother. 'Tis a pity you cannot change allegiance to a more earthly lord. King Edward could use your talents." He jerked his head at his men who were now slipping into the inn. "In truth, those lads I pulled away from the fields wouldn't have raised a hand against kin and friends. They only came after I let the sun fall on a pretty coin and promised a jack of ale." He snorted. "My brother shall return the coin. I am willing enough to pay for Tostig's finest."

"I was grateful to see you," Thomas said and hoped his friend did not see him tremble. The fear he had held back now struck him with especial force. "Nute deserves praise for his courage and swift feet. I did not want to put him in danger but had no other way of sending a message to you."

The monk glanced over the crowner's shoulder at the baker's house. Or so I believed, he said to himself, and tried not to resent how Oseberne had barred the door and failed to say that he would summon the crowner. Instead of sending Nute through the mob, Thomas could have given the child safe haven inside the house.

"I will give him the sling he wants as reward and teach him how to hunt with it after this murder is solved." Ralf's eyes filled with the affection he felt for the boy.

"Was he or Oseberne the one to first bring the news of the riot?" Thomas hoped he did not betray his annoyance with the baker.

"Nute, but the baker met us outside the priory gate and confirmed that you were trapped by the mob. He himself was just
able to escape through a back window." The crowner laughed.
"I think he was displeased that the boy came first with the news.
He scowled when he saw Nute pulling me along."

"The man owns a surfeit of pride if a child's achievement
angers him."

"Oh, he softened fast enough when Nute told him how he
ran without stopping and head down to make sure he did not
fall in the uneven road. The baker smiled then, and who would
not when a lad so young takes on a man's responsibility."

Not for the first time, Thomas concluded that the crowner
would make as good father to a son as he was to his daughter.
"However it came, I am grateful word got to you. Had you not
arrived when you did, matters might have grown far beyond my
small ability to control them."

"Nothing diminishes what you did, Brother," Ralf said, then
gestured his intent to walk back to the stables. "Did you find
out who was responsible for priming that mob like a pump with
the details of Kenelm's death?"

The monk shook his head. "While I was speaking with
Adelard before the riot, Oseberne mentioned he heard women
discussing the circumstances on market day. Now that village
passions have cooled, someone might recall the source of the
tale. Whether the first rumor included the suggestion that the
Jewish family killed the man, a detail conveniently exonerating
any villager who murdered an unpopular man, I cannot say."

"I wonder whether the mob decided if the sick wife or the
terrified husband had slit Kenelm's throat."

Thomas blinked at the crowner's mocking tone.

Ralf glanced sideways at the monk, crossed himself, and
walked on without further comment.

As they approached the new stables, they saw Cuthbert drying
his legs. An uneven puddle in the dirt and a bucket sideways
on the ground close by suggested the man had been trying to
clean himself.

The moment the sergeant saw Ralf, he groaned and threw himself at the crowner's feet. "I have failed you." Cuthbert buried his face in his hands.

"You have always been loyal to me," Ralf replied, his expression sad at the humiliation this man had endured. "We may face death alone with courage, but a threat to our families will unman us all. Had I known your neighbors would threaten your loved ones, I would not have asked you to stand guard here."

He clapped a hand on the sergeant's shoulder and ordered him to rise. Not only was this man Ralf's sergeant but his bailiff, a position of responsibility won for both faithful service and competence. Nothing that had happened this day would change the crowner's mind about Cuthbert's character.

"Indeed, I now have a more important duty for you," he said with his more usual gruffness. "Take your family to my manor house and watch over my child and her nursemaid until this trouble has passed. If any man from this village dares to even breathe over one silken hair on my daughter's head, you will smite him in half or I shall later."

Cuthbert turned away, his face red with shame. He knew that no man would dare attack the crowner's manor. Ralf had just given him a haven for his family, disguised as a task that the sergeant knew was meaningless. "My family need not…"

"Those are my orders. Your family must go with you. A child cannot do without a father for so many days, and I know your wife would mourn your absence."

The sergeant's expression betrayed his longing to argue, but he chose silence instead and nodded. As they both well knew, Ralf could send his child and her nurse to the priory for safety, if there were any real danger. In any case, Cuthbert knew he must obey. It would be insolent to refuse the crowner's kind gesture.

"Go!" Ralf ordered and gently shoved the man on his way.

As he watched Cuthbert run down the path that led to his dwelling on the edge of the village, the crowner felt at a complete loss. He had no one else to guard this vulnerable Jewish family. It would take too long to send word to his brother, now in Winchester, that soldiers were needed. The men from the farms would return to their fields, and he doubted any amount of silver he could cast at their feet would tempt them to raise a hand against neighbors to protect a group they, too, despised.

Signy had made it clear that only Kenelm had been willing to shield these hated people. How could this family be kept safe until he determined whether or not Jacob ben Asser was the killer? Even if he was, the pregnant wife, her mother, and a maid must be protected from mob violence.

Ralf looked around. It would take very little to spark another riot.

The fishermen had not been part of this recent turmoil. They never left the sea until nightfall. The other villagers had now gone back to anvil, tanning pit, and barrel making, except for a few still clustered near the inn. When these saw his glare, their expressions turned sheepish and they scurried into the inn. Whatever they had been talking over, the men seemed calm, and the crowner prayed that the ale not overheat their blood again.

Ralf turned to Brother Thomas. "I must question Jacob ben Asser about the fight he had with Kenelm." He gestured in the direction of the departed sergeant. "I need a good head to help me and witness what is said. I should have asked Cuthbert…"

"You were right to send him home, Crowner. I am happy to take his place."

"I heard the tale of the argument between Kenelm and ben Asser from Signy. Had you heard of it?"

"Oseberne and his son told me as well." Although he was happy to share what he had learned about this with his friend, he chose to remain silent about the accusations against Gytha.

Ralf turned to face the stable entrance. "Jacob ben Asser!" he shouted. "In the name of King Edward, I order you to come forth."

The face of the man who emerged was as pale as a corpse, and profound fatigue had bruised the skin with black circles under his eyes. Even his back was bent like that of an old man, but his gaze at the crowner was sharp with defiance.

This man had expected to be ripped apart by the howling mob, yet he refuses to cower and still honors the king's command. Suddenly Thomas understood that, if ben Asser had killed Kenelm, he could not demand sanctuary in the priory church, clutching the altar as a Christian might. He had no such option to avoid the hangman's rope by foreswearing the realm and sailing to France. This saddened the monk, and he found himself respecting the man's courage even more.

Jacob glanced at the monk. His jaw clenched.

Thomas stretched out his hand, then dropped it. This was one who had no desire for his blessing, let alone any comforting words he might speak. He was a monk, and his very presence was menacing to one of ben Asser's faith. Although Thomas meant no ill, he now saw that he had been wrong to come with Ralf for this questioning. His presence had been misinterpreted as a threat. In an attempt to convey a peaceful intent, the monk bowed his head.

Jacob studied at the monk, then nodded almost imperceptibly in response. Looking back at the crowner, he replied, "I obey, my lord."

"You have much to answer for," Ralf said.

Jacob spread his arms. "Ask what you must. I am ready."

"Witnesses have claimed you threatened to kill Kenelm not long before he was found dead."

Jacob's lips twisted into a bitter smile. "He and I argued. Each of us exchanged hot words. Had my corpse been found, would these villagers be so eager to riot and announce that he had threatened me in like fashion? Whether my words made him angry enough to kill is something he can no longer answer. As for me, his words did not drive me to murder."

"You exchanged blows."

"We shoved each other. Nothing more."

"What caused this quarrel?"

"He did mock my faith." Jacob's look betrayed resignation. "That, by itself, is little enough if the violence suffered is only with stinging words, my lord. We have learned to turn away when those, like Kenelm, ridicule what is holy to us."

"But you did not retreat this time."

Jacob gestured with a sigh toward the stables behind him. "As I said to you before, my wife is close to her term and suffers grievously. She needs rest to keep her strength for the coming ordeal. Kenelm, like that other youth whom you sent away, would not allow her to sleep. With courtesy, I asked him to lower his voice. He…" The man's face turned red with controlled fury. "I need not repeat what he said, but he insulted my wife's virtue and raised his voice so she could not help but hear his vile words."

Ralf nodded, gesturing for the man to continue.

"It was then that I shoved him. Perhaps we did exchange some blows." He raised his arms, then let them fall to his sides.

"You did not threaten to kill him?"

"I cannot swear to any verbal restraint in that moment. I might have said such a thing, as he might have responded in like fashion to me as well. But words are but sounds, often meaning nothing, as wise men have said. Yet he is dead, and I stand before you, still breathing. Some will surely say that proves my guilt. I can only deny it, and I give you my oath that it is true."

"Have you any proof of innocence besides your oath?"

"Will you take a woman's word?"

Ralf said nothing.

"I thought not, but my wife and her mother can confirm that I did not leave them that night."

"No one else."

"No Christian man, my lord."

Thomas looked at Ralf and saw a glimpse of sympathy in his friend's eyes.

"Yet no one can say that I left the hut, either. May two negatives prove the positive that is innocence?"

Had the matter been less grave, the crowner might have laughed at the man's jest. Thomas allowed himself to smile.

"Jacob!"

The man spun around.

A white-haired woman emerged from the stable, gesturing with cruelly crippled hands. "Belia's water has broken. She will soon give birth. We must have a doctor…"

"There is none!" Jacob finally lost control, and tears poured down his cheeks.

For just a moment, Ralf forgot that this man was a murder suspect and grabbed Jacob's shoulder. "I shall send for Sister Anne from the priory hospital."

"You must not!" Jacob's voice was raw with pain. "Our child will be baptized and taken from us." He fell to his knees and began to pray in a language Thomas recognized as Hebrew.

"You would let your wife and babe die…"

Suddenly Thomas put a restraining hand on the crowner's shoulder. "Wait!" he said and drew closer to Jacob and the white-haired woman. "Did your family not come originally from Norwich?"

Belia's mother nodded.

"Sister Anne's father was a respected physician there. His name was Benedict."

Malka gasped, covering her mouth in shock. "Benedict of Norwich? My husband and I knew him well. We…" She stared at the monk. "His daughter is a nun at this priory?"

"She is also an apothecary and trained in medical wisdom by her father before he died."

Malka's eyes grew large as she placed the heel of her palms against her cheeks. Then she knelt beside Jacob. "We must let her come. I knew her father. He was a good man, and I remember this daughter when she was a child."

"She is a nun," Jacob replied in horror. He gestured at Thomas. "They, she, he will…"

"…do nothing except allow Benedict's daughter to save Belia's life and that of my grandchild. I shall remain by my daughter's side." She looked up at the monk. "Do you swear it? Give me your word that you will not strip my Belia and her child of their faith and heritage."

"I swear that we shall not baptize the child or the mother, even in the face of death and at the cost of their immortal souls," Thomas replied. It had not been his intent to say that, and his voice shook. Oddly, his heart remained at peace. He looked up at the heavens. A soft breeze from the sea touched his face. Apparently, God was not about to strike him dead over such a promise.

"Then bring Sister Anne to my child," the mother cried. "I beg you for that mercy!"

Thomas turned and ran back to the priory much faster than he thought possible.

Chapter Fifteen

Eleanor looked down from her window and watched Brother Beorn, Gytha, and Sister Anne hurry along the mill pond path toward the village. The lay brother's galloping pace was well-matched by Sister Anne's long legs, but the maid struggled to keep up.

Had their mission been less dire, the prioress might have smiled with fond amusement. Instead, her heart ached, as it always did when women faced perilous births. Although she knew the danger and pain were Eve's legacy for rebelling against God's will, she never forgot, nor quite forgave, the death of her own mother in childbed.

She turned around. "How old is the wife?"

Brother Thomas stood near her carved audience chair and held a large orange cat in his arms. As the monk absently stroked Arthur's head, this patriarch of priory felines and hero in the wars against kitchen rodents closed his eyes and purred like a kitten.

"I believe that she and Gytha may share a similar length of time on this earth," he replied after a moment and, again falling into silence, went back to petting the cat.

This time Eleanor did smile, a delight shared by the young nun in attendance who stood near the chamber door. Many feared cats, believing them to be Satan's followers. Others concluded they were merely useful in keeping mice and rats away from edible stores. Yet this monk found as much pleasure in

Eleanor's favored beast as she did herself. And, perhaps, the cat also brought him peace and comfort after the ordeal he had faced, braving the rioting villagers. She shuddered at the risk he had taken but was proud of his courage. This time, her smile reflected her admiration for the man she both sinfully and virtuously loved.

The monk looked up, his expression contrite. "Forgive me, my lady, I did not mean to offend. My thoughts had taken a strange turn, and I was calling them back."

Knowing he had caught her smile, she said: "I meant neither mockery nor censure, Brother. Indeed, I was thinking that your well regarded gentleness was matched by your courage in preaching compassion to the villagers."

He blushed with modesty, then shook his head as if dismissing any virtue in what he had done. "Your decision to send Brother Beorn to guard Jacob ben Asser's family, while his wife gives birth, was both wise and an act of great charity, my lady."

"I did not want those men whom you faced in the road to harbor the smallest doubt that this priory follows the direction of Pope Gregory. As for the choice of Brother Beorn, that was a logical one. He is a man of the village and one known rarely to suffer fools. If he stands before the entrance to the stable, scowling as is his wont, those who are tempted to breach the fragile walls may be reminded of the cherubim with their flaming swords at the gates of Eden."

Thomas chuckled but again fell silent as he continued to stroke the cat.

"Something troubles you greatly, Brother."

Realizing that the monk's attention was drifting from him, Arthur leapt out of Thomas' arms and onto the floor.

The cat's bearing as he trotted through the chamber door reminded the prioress of a manor reeve going to inspect lands for which he was responsible.

"I may have condemned a babe's soul, my lady."

Peace fled, and she felt a chill. "How so?"

"I promised Jacob ben Asser and his mother-in-law that we would not baptize the newborn child even if it were in danger of dying. The same promise was given for the babe's mother, but she is of an age to know the consequences of her deeds."

The prioress said nothing and walked back to the window.

He waited. A light breeze flowed through the chambers, the salt smell hinting that more rain would fall within a few hours. From the orchard of priory fruit trees, birds chirped loudly to herald the coming showers. He wondered how Brother Gwydo's bees were doing under his tender care and felt an odd ache in his heart when the lay brother came to mind.

At last, the prioress turned around to face the monk, her brow furrowed.

"I shall be as forthright with you as you have been with me, Brother. I suffer doubts about the efficacy of forced baptism. As a priest, you understand better than I about these matters, but surely God knows when a conversion is not truly desired."

"I agree, my lady, but we speak primarily of a child whose reason is unformed and who is therefore dependent upon the judgment of his parents. Jacob ben Asser and his family have rejected our offer of Christian salvation. That is a dangerous decision."

"We might conclude that it is better to override their will and cloak their babe's soul in a faith the parents do not own. But if the baptized child lives, both they and we know it must be taken from them. A Christian may not be raised by a Jewish family. Shall we not trust that God will have mercy on the babe and thus let the mother know she may keep her child? The anticipation of holding an infant to her breast gives a mother comfort and strength in the throes of a dangerous birthing."

"Many men would say that salvation is of the greatest importance, that the family's faith is a delusion nurtured by the Devil, and that any comfort the mother felt was born in evil." Thomas looked away. "Yet learned voices joined with mine when I made that promise regarding the child. For one, the good Thomas Aquinas, so recently taken into God's hands, spoke of a dead infant's state of eternal joy which would be untempered by knowledge of what he had lost without baptism. And St. Paul's wisdom also echoed in my soul. Is not charity the highest virtue, even above faith?"

Eleanor nodded. "I am grateful for your teaching, Brother. It may be wiser to change men's hearts by practicing love and compassion, the tenets of our faith. Should mother and babe live, due to Sister Anne's skill and the grace of God, this family may yet see the error of their beliefs and come willingly to ours."

"I shall hope for that, my lady."

"Yet I do not believe even this question of a child's soul, no matter how important, is the sole cause of that shadow veiling your eyes."

Thomas looked down at the floor. "Rumor's face is scarred with the pox of lies and envy, her speech filled with curses, but men love her nonetheless. I fear she has recently uttered a particularly vile blasphemy."

She visibly trembled. "We have always been of one mind on the need for plain speech. What have you heard, from whom, and what is your opinion of the tale?"

"While I was questioning Adelard on his reasons for wishing to take vows, he said that the world was too wicked for him. I pressed him for examples. He claimed that Evil is so rampant that those who dress in virtue during the daylight strip themselves of it to revel in sin at night."

"He named someone from the priory?"

Thomas nodded.

"It is my duty to determine verity or falsehood in such accusations."

"He claimed to have witnessed Brother Gwydo and Gytha having carnal knowledge of each other near the hut of Ivetta the Whore on the night Kenelm was killed."

Eleanor's head turned sharply as if she had been slapped.

"My lady, I do not know Brother Gwydo well, but I cannot believe that your good maid would commit such a sin." He reached out as if pleading for forgiveness. "Had the villagers not attacked Cuthbert and the family he was protecting, I would have questioned Adelard further. Under the circumstances, I could not…"

"You had no choice," Eleanor said, her voice rough with emotion. "Nor do I believe the two committed such a deed."

"With your leave, I shall question the baker's son further."

She shook her head. "Not unless it is necessary. He believes he told you the truth, or else the Devil has enchanted him with this imagining. We can only hope that he has not whispered to others besides you about the sin he claims to have witnessed."

"I do not trust him to have held his tongue. Adelard may have spread the news in the village that Kenelm and Jacob ben Asser fought the night before the guard was murdered. He, or another, suggested the Jewish family committed the crime to sully priory ground and foul our water. That was the reason the crowd attacked Cuthbert as he stood guard at the inn's new stables, and threatened him so they could attack the Jewish family."

"Do you know that Adelard is to blame?"

"I do not. When our crowner questioned some of the men after they had calmed, no one could remember where they had heard the tale. Yet how many others could have heard the arguments?"

"Mistress Signy." She raised a hand. "I do not think that she was the source of this infamy, but, if she overheard the quarrel, others might just as well."

"But surely no one else witnessed Brother Gwydo…"

"Let us hope Adelard said nothing. If not, the reputations of both my maid and our lay brother have been rudely compromised. I must find out the truth, and we shall make sure that the innocent are cleansed of any filth thrown upon them by these lies."

"Should I summon your maid from the village?"

"Gytha is assisting Sister Anne with the birth, but, when she returns, I shall question her. As for Brother Gwydo, I would hear my maid's tale before I question him. Gytha's answers may explain all, and I may not need to involve our lay brother in this vile accusation."

With those words, Eleanor gently dismissed the monk, sending him to the inn until it was time to escort Sister Anne back to the priory, but she was deeply troubled.

Was Adelard right? Was this the cause of Gytha's sad demeanor of late? But why had the young woman not confided in her? "She must know that I would neither condemn nor cast her forth," she murmured. "After all these years, she has surely learned to trust me. Something has indeed happened, but I cannot believe the truth matches the tale Adelard has told."

Nonetheless, Eleanor retreated to her prie-dieu and, for a very long time, knelt in anxious prayer.

Chapter Sixteen

Belia's eyes were white with terror. Bloodstains streaked her chemise.

"Be brave, my sweet child and my heart's delight. This present agony is the worst," Malka crooned. "It shall not last much longer." Wiping her daughter's face with a damp cloth, she encouraged Belia to continue walking in a tight circle within the stall.

Signy pushed aside the heavy sacking over the entrance and slipped into the small space. "Do you want more water in which to bathe her?"

"The one soaking was sufficient. The boiled fenugreek, mallow, and barley need only be used at the beginning of the birth." Anne gestured at the sacking. "But please take down that cloth. The men will keep their distance while she is giving birth, and we can hardly breathe." She was sweating, and her robe was splotched with pale blood.

The innkeeper pulled it down and set it folded on the straw. "Jew or Christian, we are all daughters of Eve," she said, gesturing at mother and daughter. "Tell me what I can do to help this suffering cousin."

With anyone else, Anne might have been surprised at such words, but these came from a woman known for compassion. "I shall need more hot water in which to soak the fennel for the poultice against her back. But first I ask that you support Mistress Belia while she walks. I must speak with her mother."

Her voice must have betrayed anxiety, for sharpened fear glistened in the pregnant woman's eyes. "It is customary, before the birth, to seek knowledge only a mother can give about her child," Anne quickly added, knowing it was a lie but not a sinful one.

Signy walked over to Malka and put a gentle hand on her shoulder. "I can relieve you," she said. Then she gave the panting younger woman a brief smile. "Should the babe arrive while they are just outside, I think your mother and Sister Anne will learn the news soon enough from us both."

Belia's lips twitched with weak amusement.

For an instant Malka looked askance at the innkeeper. Then she nodded and murmured her thanks.

Taking the older woman by the arm, Anne pulled her toward the entrance. "We shall inform your husband about your progress," she said over her shoulder to the daughter. "He will be eager to learn that his child's birth is imminent."

Bracing the young woman, Signy urged her forward and began a distracting conversation. "Was the bathwater I sent warm enough?" she asked.

Outside in the courtyard, Anne carefully hid her stained hands, then realized the gesture was futile. She could do nothing about the marks on her robe.

Jacob rose, his pleading eyes dark with worry.

"Nothing has yet happened," she replied and forced a confident smile. "The birth is her first. They often take longer."

He sat down but kept his eyes on her, rejecting an answer so obviously meant to placate.

A man not easily fooled, she thought, and turned her back to him while bending close to Malka's ear. "The child is turned badly in her womb," she whispered. "I am not sure I can move it so your daughter is able to give birth."

"She will die?" Malka murmured hoarsely and turned gray. Then her mouth set with fierce determination. "She shall not." Stepping back, the mother laid her crippled hand against the nun's damp cheek. "Your father would never have allowed that. You are his daughter. I expect no less from you."

Anne stiffened, and then met the woman's steady gaze. "I will do my best. She is near the end of a woman's endurance, and her suffering will increase. All births are dangerous, but survival when the babe is twisted in the womb…" She drew in a deep breath. "Both your daughter and the child may die, although one might be saved. Do you not think we should tell her husband?"

"You shall succeed in saving her."

Anne hesitated but realized she had also been told the choice to make if only the mother or child could live. Bowing her head, she walked back to the stall. There was no time to argue.

Malka gestured to Gytha who stood nearby. "We need more hot water!"

The maid raced toward the inn's cooking hut where a large pot of rain water was kept simmering at Signy's orders. The steam struggled to rise in the heavy summer air.

When Gytha delivered the water, Anne poured some into a basin and explained to the young woman how to soak and wring the poultice. Then she sent the maid outside and began instructing Signy on what must come next.

The two women stripped Belia, and Anne showed her how to squat in the fresh straw. After washing her hands as her father had taught her, the nun picked up a bowl and a beaker filled with oil. She knelt in front of the young woman, poured the fenugreek and linen seed infused oil over her hands and began to rub it on Belia's huge belly, thighs, and pudenda.

Gytha rushed in and passed a damp linen pouch to the innkeeper.

"Does this warmth give you ease?" Signy asked, pressing the moist packet of herbs against the young woman's back as she embraced her to give support.

Belia groaned.

Quickly, Anne felt around the belly, seeking better knowledge of how the baby lay. Firmly, she pressed against the sides of where she believed the child to be and twisted.

It moved.

Belia howled.

Again, Anne twisted the unseen shape, gritting her teeth against her own terror and the pain she knew this young woman was suffering

Sobbing, Belia gazed at the ceiling.

Anne looked at Signy and nodded, then twisted once more.

The innkeeper gripped the woman tighter under her swollen breasts and began whispering in her ear.

Her back pressed against the stable wall, Malka murmured a prayer.

Pouring more oil on her hands, Anne reached between the woman's legs and measured how much the birth canal had expanded. "Belia, this will hurt," she said. "Scream if you must but save your strength for pushing the babe into the world when I command it. It won't take much longer." And may God make my words true, the nun prayed.

She eased her hand inside and felt two feet near the opening. She had not managed to turn the babe completely but did feel movement against her fingers. If only the womb would not shut before the head was free, strangling the child.

The feet emerged. She grasped them with one hand and waited, placing a palm against the belly to feel for contractions.

"Push!"

Belia screamed, her agony ripping through the thick air.

Malka pressed her bent fingers against her mouth.

"Mother!" Belia howled.

"Push!" Anne ordered, resisting all desire to wrench the child into the world. Many did, destroying both mother and child, but she felt as if her father's spirit was hovering nearby, whispering instructions and urging patience.

"Push, beloved," Malka urged with feigned confidence.

Blood now rushed through Anne's hands. This is too much bleeding, too much.

Belia strained to obey. The stall reeked with sour sweat and the metallic tang of blood. Signy hugged the woman tighter and stared at the nun.

Anne looked up at the tortured face of the exhausted Belia. "Push," she said, her voice soft and trembling. "Your child wills it."

The young woman raised her eyes and screamed, willing her body to make one final effort. With no strength left, she collapsed in Signy's arms.

Malka began to weep and reached out to touch her motionless daughter.

All voices fell silent. The rustling of Anne moving in the straw was the only sound.

Then Belia moaned, and Signy eased her backward with a sigh.

Suddenly a cry rent the air, rising in pitch. Whether meant as anguish or outrage, it issued from the tiny mouth of a baby boy.

Chapter Seventeen

Oseberne struck his son.

Adelard fell backward and just caught himself before his head hit the edge of the table. Shocked at the blow, he put a hand to his cheek, then stared at the blood mixed with tears on his fingers.

"How dare you lose that precious object?"

"The cord must have broken…"

"When did you last see the cross?" Oseberne turned his back to his son, lifted the pitcher, and poured himself a cup of wine. He offered none to Adelard.

"I had it just before Brother Thomas arrived to question me. I know because I kissed it so God might give me strength and a swift tongue."

"Afterward?"

Adelard began to weep. "I do not know! Maybe I lost it in the street when I went to join those seeking to kill the Jews."

"A silver cross, lost in the street, to be picked up by some villain." Oseberne spun around and pointed a shaking finger at his son. "Do you have any idea what that cost me?"

"I shall repay you!" The young man knelt and stretched his hands toward his father. His eyes were wide with impotent misery.

"That cross was my gift, so that you might stand without shame in the choir of monks at Tyndal Priory next to sons of higher birth." The baker gulped his wine and poured another cup. "Repay me?" he roared. "You owe me a far greater debt than the cross. The priory is your best hope of advancement on earth as well as in heaven. And have I not worked hard for this? Do I not deserve an obedient son in God's service, one who would spend his life praying for my soul?" Sneering, he continued. "Dare you be so ungrateful as to force my soul to suffer in Purgatory when it could be quickly freed from its agonies by filial devotion?"

"And my mother's soul," Adelard whispered.

"A wife who took nun's vows? She's in Heaven and has no need of our prayers." Oseberne wiped a hand across his mouth. "And now you think you can crawl into that priory like some freedman's son." He looked heavenward. "Prior Andrew may not even accept you. I would not blame him, careless and ungrateful wretch that you are."

Adelard covered his face.

"And all you do is whine." His face red with anger, the baker grabbed a handful of his son's hair and pulled his head back. "Ever since those cowards failed to punish that family of Jews for the crimes they have done and hope to commit, you have been bleating like a woman with her courses." Bending down, he spat in his son's face. "You are unmanned. Why?"

"I have sinned!"

"That you have. Most certainly against me for losing the silver cross, a crime you failed to confess until I discovered it."

"Another evil yet."

Letting go of his son's head, Oseberne stared at the lad. "What else could be so heinous? Surely you have not lain with some pocky girl and seeded a bastard?"

Adelard shook his head, exuding a horror that matched his father's disgust. "Worse! I have gone against the teachings of the saints and God."

Oseberne stepped back, both worried and perplexed. "And what will this cost me?"

Staggering to his feet, the young man looked longingly at the wine jug.

His father ignored the hint. "Out with it! What have you done?"

"Brother Thomas told us all, as we gathered about the inn stables where the Jews stay, that when St. Bernard of Clairvaux preached the crusade, he forbade good Christians to harm those Jews living there." He raised a trembling hand to keep his father from interrupting him. "And the good monk also quoted from a letter written by Pope Gregory, stating that the tales of these people drinking the blood of Christian children were untrue."

Oseberne waved the words away. "Blasphemy."

The son murmured a weak protest.

"At my most charitable, I shall say that this monk is sinfully ill-informed. The priest who taught me was firm in the belief that the world shall never be truly Christian until we sweep the earth clean of all unbelievers. What difference is there between those infidels who stole Jerusalem for their wicked purposes and the Jews who killed Our Lord?"

Adelard mumbled in confusion.

"Shall you trust Brother Thomas, a man who lacked a faith strong enough to keep him in his hermitage? Dare you take his word over mine, a man taught by one so holy that he never removed his hair shirt even when his skin rotted and dropped from his body?"

"I have always followed your teaching, but you have also directed me to take holy vows and enter Tyndal Priory so I might pray for your soul's peace after death. There I shall meet Brother Thomas again, a man who may well become my confessor."

"Then find a holier one than he for that. Seek a man who reeks with contempt for the world. Brother Thomas spends too much time with the secular sons of Adam, and for this reason, amongst others, I doubt his virtue."

Adelard opened his mouth to speak, then drew back in fear as his father bent so close that he could count protruding nose hairs.

"Does scripture not demand that you honor, obey, and treat me with due reverence?"

His son nodded.

"I do not doubt that Brother Thomas has some benighted reason for spewing blasphemy and suggesting his foul lies were uttered by holier men than he. Did you ever see for yourself any proof that these letters came from the pope or the saint?"

Adelard shook his head.

"The Devil is clever with his tricks, often quoting events and letters that are only the spawn of hellish fantasy."

"Aye, but…"

"Have you heard these tales before Brother Thomas spoke of them?"

"Never." The young man began to bite at his knuckle.

"Then you do not know if they ever existed. Oseberne straightened his back and folded his muscular arms. "I would say that your greatest sin is to question my teaching."

Wiping his hand on his robe, Adelard protested that he had never doubted his father.

"Have I not warned you about the wicked nature of women, creatures that caused Adam to be cast out of Eden and to this day lure his sons into sin? And have you not learned the truth of my teaching through your own observations?"

"Of course, but then why urge me to join an Order run by Eve's daughter?" The youth stepped back as if fearing a blow for daring to ask.

Although Oseberne's eyes narrowed, he only raised his fist at his son. "She is the daughter of a baron who found favor with King Henry. Her brother stands by King Edward's side. If you serve her well, she may speak favorably of you to her well-regarded kin. In such cases, men have been granted small monasteries to lead. Or else I may profit from any favor you earn by gaining more business. I have offered a donation of bread to the hospital. Perhaps the priory will buy more, rather than having nuns bake when they should be praying for a soul."

The young man lowered his head, the gesture suggesting he was humbled. A renewed sniffling reinforced the impression.

Oseberne smiled down at his eldest son, his eyes glittering with the expectation of an abject apology.

Suddenly, Adelard straightened and marched toward the door. "I must seek Brother Thomas," he said, "and question him further about his meaning and ask for proof of his allegations. Surely you agree that I dare not reject the words if they prove true, but if he lies, the village must hear of it. The Jews cannot live if Satan protects them."

Oseberne stared, rendered speechless by the unexpected intensity of this son's gaze.

Adelard swung open the door and left the house.

Just as the door closed, Oseberne threw a pottery cup against the wall. It shattered into tiny pieces of clay and scattered across the floor, dotting the rushes with drops of scarlet wine.

Chapter Eighteen

Sister Anne sipped at a mazer of wine. "After we bathed and swaddled the babe, we called Master Jacob to see his son." She ran a finger around the edge of the cup. "The child roared like a lion, but the new father stroked his son's face as if the boy were a kitten." Sadness swept across her face but lasted only as long as a wind-driven mist.

"His cry of joy pleased both his wife and Mistress Malka," Gytha said, offering more wine.

Anne nodded. "Had it not been forbidden, he would have kissed the new mother in gratitude for the gift she gave him."

"I did not understand why he kept such a distance," Gytha said.

"The tenets of his faith forbade him to touch her after the birthing," the nun replied and quickly turned to the prioress.

"How fares Mistress Belia?" Eleanor's question showed concern for the young woman, but her troubled look was directed toward her maid.

"She suffered more than most, and it is a miracle that both she and the child survived." Anne shook her head. "All danger has not yet passed. I pray she will continue to gather strength as she is now. After the difficulties of this birth, it is likely she will never bear another child. At least her bleeding stopped, and the afterbirth was soon expelled. Of course she had chills but that is normal."

"I am grateful to you both," the prioress said, "as the family must be as well."

"My efforts were petty, but Mistress Signy assisted most," Gytha said. She had drunk only a little of her wine before she set the mazer back on the table.

"Indeed!" Eleanor's smile suggested this was not a surprise.

"I had only asked her to warm a bath for Mistress Belia, before the contractions grew too frequent, and she made sure the required herbs were well-infused. But later she insisted on helping to support the mother and massage her back. As she explained to me, she might not have birthed a child but she was still a daughter of Eve like us all."

"Our innkeeper is a good woman," Eleanor said. "I have known few others who understand the meaning of charity so well."

"Where is Brother Thomas?" the sub-infirmarian asked. "He accompanied us back from the inn, but I have not seen him at the hospital."

"He has gone to seek Brother Gwydo. Prior Andrew has not seen our lay brother since yesterday but assumes the bees had kept him from the Offices. I must ask him some questions about Kenelm's murder."

Gytha paled.

Anne, who had seen the same response, glanced at the prioress. "If you will permit me, I should return to the hospital," she said. "If I am needed again by Mistress Belia…"

"You must go to her at once."

Smiling, the nun departed.

Eleanor laid a gentle hand on her maid's shoulder. "Stay with me, my child. We must talk."

"I have feared this," Gytha whispered.

Although she would have preferred to embrace the young woman and offer comfort, Eleanor believed she must put a formal distance between them if she were to seek truth without bias. As she sat in her carved chair and indicated that her maid must stand before her, she felt cruel and hated it. Only rarely had she insisted on such formality between them.

The young woman covered her eyes. "I have sinned, my lady. I have been so wicked that I contaminate all within the priory. Indeed, I have dishonored you by failing to confess what I have done and should have left your service…"

"You shall not leave my side until you marry," Eleanor replied, then gestured at the abandoned mazer on the table. Her resolve to remain stern was already faltering. "Drink that for strength while you tell me what happened the night you returned from visiting Tostig. After all the years you have served me, and the love I bear you, do you think I would listen without compassion? What occurred between you two?" She deliberately left half of the pair unnamed.

"You have suspected the truth?" Shock briefly drifted across Gytha's face, then dissipated. "I should never have doubted it. Anytime in the past, when I wished to hide something from you, I knew I would fail and therefore admitted all. This time, however…" Her voice failed and she looked away.

"Bring that stool and sit beside me, my child," Eleanor sighed, unable to restrain her feelings any longer. "I must hear the tale from you." Although she doubted that her maid had lain with Gwydo, she found herself wishing that they had. That transgression was arguably within her authority to judge and order penance. But something whispered in her ear that Kenelm's murder must be involved. The man's death and Adelard's tale of the coupling were too coincidental in time and place.

Gytha took a deep breath, looked down at the wine, and swallowed half of it. "After I left my brother, I stopped to visit with Signy and then came back to the priory. Kenelm followed me, but I did not notice him until I was close by the mill gate. He grabbed my arm and forced a kiss." She shuddered.

The prioress let silence take on the weight of her growing apprehension.

"When I struggled, he clasped a hand over my mouth and dragged me into the forest."

"You feared rape."

"With cause, my lady. Just off the road, I tripped. He fell on me and tried to thrust himself between my legs." She squeezed her eyes shut and took a deep breath. "God heard my prayers. I found a stone with which I struck his head with all my strength. Then I was able to pull myself away."

"He did not…"

"I remained a virgin but at a deadly price."

Eleanor reached out and touched her maid's cheek with sympathy. All this had happened in the forest, she realized. Kenelm had not been on priory grounds.

"He lay still and his head was bleeding," Gytha continued, "but I was terrified, both of him and what I had done. All reason fled, and I ran deeper into the forest. Then I fell down the embankment. I must have struck my head, for I remember nothing more until I awoke."

"Do you know how long you were senseless?"

"Nay, but when I recovered, Brother Gwydo was kneeling next to me."

"What did he do or say?" The prioress studied Gytha's face for signs of unease but saw none. Had Adelard witnessed just this, his overheated imagination might have concluded they had lain together. Or could he have seen Kenelm wrestling with the maid on the ground instead and, seeing Gwydo a short time later, assumed the two men were one?

Eleanor was perplexed. There was no reason for the baker's son to conclude it was Gwydo he had seen when it was Kenelm. If there was light enough to see anything, the youth could have told the difference between the short but stocky former soldier and the tall, broad-shouldered stranger.

"Nothing dishonorable, my lady." Gytha flushed. "He asked if I could stand and assisted me when I struggled. Then he led me to the mill gate." She pressed her fingers to her eyes. "I think he asked if I could go the rest of the way by myself but I am not sure. I cannot recollect, but I was alone by the time I climbed the stairs to your chambers."

"You said nothing of this to anyone before now."

"I did not. The hour was late. You had gone to bed. I lay down and tried to sleep. The memory of all that happened was both too vivid and too much like a dream. I neither had the courage to speak of it, nor did I know how to do so. Then Kenelm's body was found..."

Not in the forest but in our mill pond, the prioress added to herself. "When Brother Gwydo took you to the priory gate, did you remember if you passed by the spot where Kenelm lay?"

Gytha shook her head.

"Did you tell our lay brother what had happened to you?"

"I doubt it, my lady, for I was ashamed, but I cannot recall."

And where might the lay brother have been going that would have precluded him from taking her to the hospital or otherwise seeking care? Perhaps he had seen Kenelm attack Gytha and witnessed her flight into the forest. That would excuse his departure from priory grounds if he sought to help her. It would not explain why he had failed to make sure Sister Anne examined her.

"I killed Kenelm, my lady!"

"Yet his body was found in the mill pond, not in the forest where you left him. You must be honest with me, for I shall do all I can to help. Did you and Brother Gwydo drag his body into our priory grounds and push it into the stream?"

Gytha put her hands over her face, fighting to recover her memory. Then she shook her head. "All I recall is walking through the gate, then nothing more until I was climbing the stairs to your chambers. I cannot swear an oath that we did not do such a thing; neither can I say we did."

"You do not remember seeing Kenelm again?"

"I can recollect nothing about him at all after I fell down the bank."

"Do you recall whether Brother Gwydo followed you back into the priory?"

Gytha hesitated, then suddenly looked horrified. "Might he have seen Kenelm lying on me, witnessed the killing, and tried to hide my sins by throwing the corpse into the mill pond?"

Eleanor leaned back in her chair. He might have done so. She would question him about it as well as the reason he was outside the priory. Although she could not completely dismiss the possibility that her maid had killed Kenelm with the blow to the head, Anne had not believed the wound to be fatal. In any case, she did not think Gytha was lying to her, nor did she think the maid had deliberately left anything out of her tale.

One crucial question remained unanswered: who had slit the man's throat and why? Gytha had not mentioned this detail, and Eleanor knew the evidence suggested that Kenelm had suffered the certain fatal wound after the blow to his head.

"My lady?"

"Forgive me. I do not know if the lay brother did as you suggested. When Brother Thomas brings him to me, I shall question him about this."

Gytha looked away. "I regret any sorrow I have brought on him. He was kind to me when I needed aid, and no one here has ever spoken ill of him."

"I shall not forget his gentler nature. Should any rebuke be required, it will be for something he took upon himself."

"But surely you cannot keep me in your service if I killed a man, my lady." The maid's face was pale, but she stiffened with resolve. "I will accept the punishment I am due."

"Of course, you will continue to serve me. You struck a man who did violence against you. For that, I find no fault that cannot be cleansed through confession. Yet I must still summon Crowner Ralf." She bent forward and took Gytha's hand in hers. "You are obliged to tell him your tale as well, my child, but we both know him to be a just man."

What she omitted saying was that the king might not find reason for clemency if Gytha were judged guilty of Kenelm's death, even if she protested that the deed was committed to protect her virtue. Other than the possibility of Brother Gwydo, there were no witnesses who could confirm the truth of her allegation. If asked, Adelard would say he had seen the maid and lay brother together and swear he had observed sinful pleasure.

That would destroy Gytha's claim to chastity and any statement by Brother Gwydo. The only hope was that the one who slit Kenelm's throat could be found.

Although the maid was not under the Church's authority, the prioress decided she would beg the king's leniency should Gytha be found guilty of murder. King Edward would set a price for such mercy, and Eleanor now swore a silent oath to pay it.

Gytha nodded and fell silent. Her expression spoke of both grief and resignation.

Chapter Nineteen

Eleanor watched her maid and the crowner look away from each other. Had she not already concluded that the love between them had grown to the point of imminent confession, she would have known it now. Sadly, this encounter would be a far less joyful moment. She grieved for the pain both must be enduring.

Ralf cleared his throat. "I must speak with Mistress Gytha alone, my lady."

Gytha turned to look at the prioress, her eyes begging for the mercy of Eleanor's company.

The prioress nodded with an equal measure of reluctance and firmness. "I know you must, crowner. But I shall remain in my private chamber, with the door left open for propriety. There is no one else who could be spared to attend this interview, the details of which we all pray shall remain private." A lie, of course, and surely he knew it, but after all these years of friendship, she had learned to read his face well. He did not want her completely absent, any more than Gytha did, and none of them wanted to chance disclosure by another about what would be spoken here.

As expected, he muttered concurrence.

Folding her hands into her sleeves, she looked up at Ralf, her expression stern. "No matter what you resolve to do after hearing what Mistress Gytha has to say, be advised that I shall defend her with every means at my disposal."

"I would expect no less, my lady." Ralf's demeanor was formal, but his voice shook.

"Nor shall you take her from this priory. I give you my sacred oath that she will arrive when summoned for trial, if such be needed, but I will not have her dishonored by confinement in some foul prison cell."

"Were it necessary to place Mistress Gytha under arrest, I myself would beg you for that mercy you have just offered."

"Then I shall go to my chambers." As she passed by her maid, the prioress stopped and drew the young woman into her arms. "I believe you to be innocent of any crime," she murmured, "and Crowner Ralf will surely concur. He must do his duty, my child, but do not think he takes any pleasure in this."

Gytha held onto Eleanor for a long moment and then drew back, raising her chin with proud determination.

"Be honest with him. There may be something in what you recall that will give him a detail needed to capture the one who did kill Kenelm." Quickly, she kissed her maid's cheek and blessed her. "Have courage!"

Gytha watched the prioress walk from the room, then turned to face the crowner, her expression like that of a woman irrevocably facing her executioner, alone and struggling to retain her dignity.

"Mistress Gytha, I must ask you to repeat all you have told Prioress Eleanor."

Pale, but voice firm, she did.

Ralf did not once interrupt, but his face turned red and his eyes narrowed. When Gytha had finished, he turned his back on her and strode to the window.

Gytha waited, then trembled with growing anxiety.

He ground his fist into the stones of the wall. "If Kenelm raped you…"

"I remain a virgin." Her voice cracked. "On that matter, I give you my oath."

"But he forced himself on you! Kenelm was strong, a large man. How could you have had time to strike him with the rock before he…?"

"I did, but I did not mean to kill him. I only wanted to save my honor."

"A fine hope!" He spun around and shouted: "But I cannot believe you stopped him in time."

Gytha's eyes widened.

"He deserved to die for destroying your chastity!"

"He succeeded only in bruising and frightening me." Confusion mixed with anger sharpened her tone. "Do not make a mockery of my plight. My sin is a killing that I swear was never intended. Why shout so about a loss that did not occur?"

He shook his head.

Gytha's face turned scarlet. "Oh, now I see what you are about, my lord. You have decided my guilt. My oath is without merit because I am a woman, and you grieve that Tostig's sister must now be called a *whore!*"

"I can defend you against the murder," he replied, "but you cannot recover..." The crowner covered his eyes.

Anger flashed from hers.

He opened his hands to plead with her. "How can I believe that Kenelm did not violate you? It is against all logic."

She stepped back from him. "For all your flaws, my lord, I have always called you a just man. Sadly, I find that you are no different from any other, all of whom believe women are besotted with lust. Perhaps you have also concluded that I seduced Kenelm, then struck him so he would not tell how I forced him to couple with me?"

"I do not..."

"In truth," she shouted, "do not all men demand that their wives bloody the nuptial sheet while they mount other women without a thought to any consequences? And should a man shatter a woman's virginity without her consent, you, like any son of Adam, cast the woman aside, claiming that the rapist erred only in failing to pray hard enough for the strength to resist her wiles."

"Gytha!" He slammed his fist against the wooden table and howled with pain.

"Enough!" Eleanor strode into the room. "This woman has been as loyal to me and shown as much love as any who shared my mother's womb. For that, I respect the truth of her words and shall shield her against all who dare to point condemning fingers." She glared at Ralf. "And you? You have known her since she was a child and call her brother your closest friend. Surely you owe her even greater loyalty than I, crowner." Walking over to Gytha, she pulled her close to her side. "This interrogation has ended."

The crowner nodded and looked away.

"Leave us, my child," Eleanor said. "He has heard your story, and we have agreed that you shall remain here no matter what he concludes. Seek peace in the cloister garth until I come for you." Shooting a barbed look at Ralf, she added, "I must speak with this man a brief moment longer."

Her eyes moist with repressed grief, Gytha fled the chambers, slamming the door behind her.

Eleanor was now alone with a man, against all rules. For once, she was too angry to care. "You should be ashamed, Ralf. I would not have urged her to speak with you had I known you would have treated her with such disregard. You have betrayed my trust."

He fell to his knees in front of her.

"Oh, stand up," she said and turned to the table. Pouring two cups of wine, she pushed one into the crowner's hand.

He drained the cup.

She poured him more. "You, as well as I, love Gytha, yet you have deeply wounded her. My trust may have been betrayed, but your brutal words to her are the greater sin. How dare you doubt her honor and accuse her of lying when she swore she had not been raped. That was more than cruel. That was the act of one in whom God had failed to place a heart."

He looked like a man facing an eternity in Hell.

"I must forgive the insult to me, because my vows require it, but I am not obliged to forget the wound you inflicted on a good woman." The prioress glared at him. "Even assuming she had been raped, surely you know that she would never marry you until she knew she would not quicken with Kenelm's foul seed. And if proof of virginity is truly required, should she ever be willing to let you take her to the church door, Sister Anne will provide it." She threw up her hands in disgust. "What were you thinking, Ralf! Or were you thinking at all?"

"God has cursed me with lack of wit," he groaned. "It is not the first time I have spoken so rudely."

"Indeed, it is not," the prioress snapped. "This time you shall pay dearly for it."

Silence fell between them, then Eleanor walked to him and lightly put her hand on his arm. "Aye, you have stabbed her to the heart. Whether or not the blow is fatal we cannot yet know, nor dare we take the time now to consider a possible remedy. For Gytha's sake as well, the murder must be solved first." Retreating to a proper distance, the prioress asked: "Do you think it possible that Gytha killed Kenelm even in the defense of her honor?"

"Nay," he said without hesitation and swallowed the remaining wine. "Nor, as you told me, does Sister Anne."

"Neither do I." She pointed to the jug.

He hesitated.

She smiled and poured again. "Someone cut his throat. I did not mention that detail to Gytha. She claims that she only hit him with a rock and that must have killed him. There is no reason for her to hide another wound when she has already confessed to the murder."

He agreed, then sipped with moderation.

"As we discussed before you were summoned to the riot, there was blood in the ground above the mill. According to Sister Anne, a man bleeds only before death."

"That means that someone discovered Kenelm still alive, dragged him to the mill, slit his throat, and threw the body in."

"Or perhaps found him after he dragged himself inside the gate and then cut the man's throat. That is probably a minor difference, so I say we are in agreement. Unfortunately, we have only Gytha's confession about striking the man. Unless we find the true killer, suspicion will continue to cloak her." She raised a hand to stop him from speaking. "Even if she is found innocent because of the circumstances, Ralf, some will always condemn her for the violence unless another is hanged for the murder."

"That cur, Adelard, will never shut his mouth about it," the crowner growled.

"As Gytha's tale points out, there is one more element in this vile tale that must be resolved." Eleanor's expression was grim. "Brother Thomas is seeking Brother Gwydo now. When he brings him to me, I will ask why he was outside the priory, how he discovered Gytha, if he saw Kenelm or anyone else, and what he did after her took her to the mill gate."

"Do you think the lay brother killed Kenelm?"

"I cannot conclude anything before I question him, Ralf."

"And you must do so without me."

"He is under my leadership and the Church's rule."

The crowner bowed his head. "I know you will share with me whatever you discover, my lady." He took a deep breath. "As for Mistress Gytha and the wrong I have done unto her..."

"When this other crime has been solved, Ralf, I shall do all I can to bridge the chasm between you. It is a wide one," she said, then shook her head. "But differences can often be resolved and loving hearts bonded more firmly with the wisdom learned in the struggle. Pray, as shall I, that this may be true for you both."

Chapter Twenty

Frowning, the young lay brother leaned on his hoe. "Nay, I have not seen Brother Gwydo since yesterday."

Thomas was now worried. "Did you speak with him then?"

"I told him what I knew about the riot in the village. Did you not hear the shouting?"

"I was there," the monk replied. "How did you learn of it?"

"I pulled myself up on the mill gate and asked a passerby on the road." The youth flushed. "On the vows I have taken, Brother, I swear I was only a hand's breadth outside the wall." But curiosity still sparkled in his eyes. "What more have you learned?" the youth whispered. "Were the Jews killed?"

"No." Thomas had neither the time nor the inclination to give details. "How did Brother Gwydo respond?"

The lay brother looked sufficiently chastened. "He was unhappy, saying that this violence was a wicked thing. When I asked why he was so troubled by it, he said nothing more but left and walked back toward his bees." The lay brother shook his head. "Why would he have said that? Hadn't he gone on pilgrimage to Outremer to recover Jerusalem from the infidels? Are Jews not infidels?"

Thomas was even less eager to repeat his sermon to the villagers on the rights of the king's people than he was to trade tales. He had to find Gwydo. "I will send for you later and explain the Church's position on those of Jewish faith."

The man's expression suggested less than enthusiastic anticipation.

Leaving the lay brother to his struggles with the garden weeds, Thomas strode down the path that led to the mill. Where had Gwydo gone?

He had already searched the priory. The man was not in the dormitory, nor had he fallen ill and gone to the hospital. Only Brother John was in the chapel, a man who constantly begged God to pardon frailties he could never forgive himself.

Reaching the mill pond, Thomas slid down the embankment and found a full pottery jug left in the water. He pulled himself back up to the path and walked toward the skeps. As the buzzing grew louder, he looked around. No one was tending the bees.

"What do I even know about the man?" Thomas asked himself as he left the clearing. Had Gwydo been married, and did he have children? Where was he from, and what was his parentage? He did have a singing voice the seraphim would envy, and Thomas felt at ease with him.

That last thought gave him pause.

He rarely let down his guard with others. Oh, a few to be sure, but they shared his feeling of not quite fitting into the world as most did. Prior Andrew, for instance, had fought on the wrong side of the de Montfort rebellion. Sister Anne had followed her beloved husband to the priory, despite having no longing for the cloister herself. Never did he have cause to doubt Gwydo's sincere faith and calling, but he had sensed a profound sorrow hiding deep in the man's soul, a feeling he himself understood well.

He continued through the mill gate and walked into the road. For want of a better destination in his hunt, he decided to visit the place known as the hut of Ivetta the Whore, where he had spent almost a year as a hermit.

The sea breeze was soft and carried a welcoming coolness to the land. Had yesterday not brought a village near riot and a family close to death, the world might have been as sweet and innocent as it was only a day after God finished creating it.

Thomas shook his head. This illusion was surely the Devil's mockery. A man's throat had been slit, and the stench of hatred was still in the air. Slipping into the forest, he stepped over a rotting log and found the short-cut to the hut.

He had not walked far before he saw where someone might have tripped and tumbled down the embankment. Kneeling on the ground, he found a root pulled up, the earth still damp where it had been buried, and the surrounding vegetation flattened or broken. He bent over the edge and concluded that the distance to the stream was not far. There were many rocks and some tree trunks that could break any fall but which also might break an arm or injure a head.

Was Gwydo lying wounded and helpless below? He eased himself down to the water's edge.

A brief search of the area revealed neither lay brother nor anything else of note. Thomas sighed with frustration and climbed back up.

He loved this forest, a place apart where he had often mused without interruption in his days as a hermit. Of course it held danger as well. There were often rumors of lawless men, although he had never seen them, and near the stream below he had once found a body. Here too, Gytha and the lay brother had been seen by Adelard.

Of course he was certain that the prioress' maid was innocent of any intentional sin. As for Gwydo's reasons for being outside the priory, blameless or culpable, Thomas worried that his ignorance of the man's past kept him from grasping what the lay brother's true involvement was.

The first question to consider was whether or not Adelard was correct in believing he had seen the lay brother and Gytha coupling. Had the current situation been less dire, the monk would have laughed at the absurdity of the allegation. After all, he had known the prioress' maid from the time she was just past childhood.

A woman vowed to God could not be more chaste. It was common enough for young village women to lie with lovers, often bearing large bellies to the church door as an additional witness to the joyful union, but Gytha had not done so. Her fondness for the crowner and his little daughter was well known, but Ralf had never tried to take advantage of that either, despite loving her in return. All of Tyndal knew how he felt. Some had even wagered on when he might finally ask her to marry him.

Why, then, would she lie with Gwydo?

Or had he raped her?

He entered the small clearing where the hut stood and paused for a moment, feeling a twinge of sadness. Prioress Eleanor had taken permanent possession of this small bit of land for the priory and ordered it tended until another monk begged for a hermit's retreat. Thomas wondered if she was thinking of Brother John, who was steadily withdrawing from the mortal world.

In the meantime, he was pleased that his old vegetable garden was still being cultivated and the hut kept in good repair by a man in Tostig's employ. He took a deep breath, taking the opportunity to draw in some of the peace he still found here. Then he sat on the wooden bench he had built and pulled his mind back to Gwydo.

Was the man likely to have raped any woman, let alone the prioress' maid?

Although Thomas never claimed his opinions were infallible, he strongly doubted the former soldier had done so. One of the reasons he was comfortable in the company of this lay brother was the man's profound gentleness. Gwydo may have been a soldier, and surely killed men in battle, but he had often said that war had given him a calling for peace. Clenching his fist with the agony of memory, Thomas was quite aware that rape was a violent act. Whatever Gwydo had done in battle, he had come to Tyndal seeking tranquility. Such a man was unlikely to defile a virgin.

If none of this occurred, had Adelard lied or simply misinterpreted what he had seen? The young man had faults enough, but he had shown willingness to listen yesterday, despite his initial enthusiasm for killing the family in the stables. That suggested there was a seed of compassion in the man's heart, or at least a crack in his otherwise rigidly defined canon of sins. Thus it seemed more likely to Thomas that Adelard had misjudged what he saw.

But that was as far as he could reason, the monk decided. He did not have enough facts. All he was going on was intuition, a woman's weakness from which he frequently suffered. "Yet I have not often been failed by it," he muttered, feeling uncomfortable and obliged to defend himself despite being alone.

Rising from the bench, he chose to visit the pond below the hut where he had once enjoyed a daily swim in summer. Perhaps, Thomas decided with little hope, he would find Gwydo snoring on the bank.

When he reached the path leading downward, he suddenly stopped.

Something was not right. He sniffed the air.

Animals often died, and perhaps that was the sweet rot of death he smelled, but the odor was pungent. He stepped cautiously into the immediate undergrowth and began to pull aside bushes and jab into piles of fallen debris.

It did not take him long to find the body.

Just a few feet from the path, Gwydo lay on his back, bulging eyes empty of meaning, lips stretched in a silent scream, and hands clenched against his neck. The lay brother had been strangled with a cord that still bit into the flesh under his chin.

Thomas knelt, bent to the corpse's ear, and whispered the ritual of forgiveness.

In a beam of sunlight, just a short distance away, something glittered and caught the monk's attention. When he took it into his hand, he realized the object was a cross. It was one made of silver.

There was no question about what the discovery meant. The last time he had seen this, it was hanging around Adelard's own neck.

Chapter Twenty-one

Sister Anne laid her hand on the head of the new corpse. Her touch was as gentle as a mother's on her son. "Garroted. From the state of rigor, signs of decay, and the last time anyone saw him, I assume the killing was probably done on the same day as the riot."

"Why did he have to be killed?" Eleanor gripped her hands tightly against her waist as if fearing she might raise a fist in anger to the heavens. "He came to our priory seeking peace. We failed him."

"He left the protection of our walls, my lady," Thomas said, his voice soft.

"That alone was a small enough failing, one I might have forgiven quickly if the cause for disobedience owned a higher virtue." She closed her eyes. "We do not know if his act was based in good or ill, but I grieve that he died without the consolation of faith."

"I pray his soul was still hovering over his corpse for I absolved him of his sins," Thomas said. "I knew little of his past life, but he was gentle enough in his current one. No man ought to face God's judgment without the chance to shed any mortal failings."

"There is no question that he shall be buried with the respect due any of our religious." The prioress turned to Ralf. "What are your thoughts on this latest death?"

The crowner swallowed as if his throat was too dry for speech.

Eleanor attempted to soften her sharply asked question with a smile. Ralf might be a rough man, often insensitive and rude, but he longed for justice as much as she. His keen wits were needed here. For this reason, more than any demand of faith, she must be kinder, despite her hot anger over what he had done to Gytha.

"Perhaps we should begin with the premise that Master Jacob might have killed Kenelm," he said tentatively.

"Yet he is innocent of this murder since our brother was probably killed yesterday when the village was howling for ben Asser's own death," Eleanor replied. "Would you agree?"

The crowner nodded. "After the riot ended, I was questioning him when his wife began her birth pains. While Brother Thomas left to seek help, I remained and am a witness to the man's presence at the inn."

"I stayed with Master Jacob while Mistress Belia suffered her travail," the monk said.

"And Brother Beorn will be able to confirm whether the adoring new father has left the stable since." Eleanor looked at Brother Thomas. "You can speak with him soon enough about that."

"Before we continue, I must add a detail about this murder that may eliminate some suspects," Anne said, pointing to the neck of the corpse. "Brother Gwydo was a strong man, albeit of average height." She glanced briefly at Ralf. "Most women would be too short and not powerful enough to do this."

Eleanor turned to Anne. "Which would eliminate any woman of, shall we say, Gytha's approximate height and strength. I believe she is similar to most women in the village?"

"Indeed."

Eleanor was sorry she had directed that minor lash of her tongue at the crowner and looked at him with evident regret.

The crowner stared at his feet. "Yet I must ask if a woman could have strangled Brother Gwydo if he had been kneeling?"

"He did not die willingly," Sister Anne said. "Two of his fingers were deeply cut where he tried to loosen the thin band around his throat. I found no earth stains on his robes that would suggest he was kneeling. Anything is possible, but I believe it most likely that a man did this."

Eleanor gestured to the crowner to let her whisper in his ear. "It was not Gytha," she murmured. "She was with Sister Anne during and after the birth of Master Jacob's son. Before that, she was in my company and returned from the village with our nun."

Ralf straightened. "You have convinced me, Annie."

"Very well, then. First, we have the murder of Kenelm, which might have been committed by Master Jacob." Eleanor nodded to the crowner. "That one might even have been committed by a woman, although the deeply slashed throat and other details make such a conclusion less likely. Second, we have Brother Gwydo's murder, which could not have been done by Master Jacob and probably not by a woman. And our lay brother would not have strangled himself any more than Kenelm would have slit his own throat."

"Unless we have two murderers, we have gone from too many suspects to none," Ralf said. "Both Brother Gwydo and Kenelm were strangers here. No one knows anything about Kenelm's past, a matter still worth more questioning. As for the lay brother, you knew most about him, my lady. We must find out why he left the priory."

"His home was once Cambridge," Eleanor said.

Ralf was surprised. "Jacob ben Asser and his family traveled from that city as well."

"Many live there," Eleanor replied, but she paused a moment. "Did he suggest he knew either our lay brother or Kenelm?"

"He did not, nor is there anything to suggest Kenelm was from Cambridge or knew the Jewish family from the past. His taunts did not indicate a dislike beyond the family's faith. As for Brother Gwydo, we should ask Master Jacob if they knew one another." Ralf gestured at the corpse. "But ben Asser could not have killed this man. I am not sure we would learn much even if the two did know each other in Cambridge."

"And I know little more about our lay brother. He had some family still living, but he begged me to leave them in ignorance of his situation. They believed he had died in Outremer. Since he was taking vows, he did not want them to say farewell twice."

"You would say if his kin had reason to kill him." Ralf knew he could not pry out more.

"An aged father, a wife, and at least one brother who would take his place as heir whether or not Brother Gwydo lived," Eleanor replied.

Ralf glanced briefly at Sister Anne. "His wife might prefer him dead if she wanted to remarry."

"So she sent someone, perhaps Kenelm, to kill him? That would be an even graver sin than adultery." The prioress shook her head. "The guard's only visit to the priory was in search of work. When refused, he was not seen here again. That said, your suggestion would be plausible, except Kenelm died first and then Brother Gwydo." She turned to Brother Thomas. "You have been quiet," she said gently. "What are you thinking? I would hear what you might have to say."

The monk's eyes refocused as her question registered. His mind had wandered some distance from those matters currently under discussion. "I fear my judgment may have been in error about one person we have not mentioned." He pulled the silver cross from his pouch. "Does anyone know the owner of this object that I recovered near our lay brother's body?"

"Adelard, the baker's son?" Ralf reached out to take the article.

"Are you sure it is his?" Eleanor asked. "If anyone else could have owned this one…"

"I first saw it when I was questioning him on his calling," Thomas said.

"And I, when I sent him off to his father to prevent a fight with Master Jacob." Ralf looked down at the cross, tilting it back and forth. When it caught the light, it glittered like raindrops in the sun. "Few in the village could afford such a fine thing. I remember hearing that his father had given him this when he first spoke of becoming a monk. Even if others might have been able to buy such a thing, no one, to my knowledge, has."

"May I?" Sister Anne held out her hand.

Ralf passed the cross to her.

"Yet I do not recall whether Adelard was wearing it when I addressed the villagers outside the inn's stables." Thomas closed his eyes as he tried to remember the details. "He stood near the front, and we did speak. The sun was shining, and the cross should have caught the light." He fell silent.

"This cross has a loop for a cord or chain." Anne looked up from examining the dead man's neck. "The cord used to strangle Brother Gwydo is knotted but could have fit through that loop." She tugged a bit of the cord loose from the corpse and studied it. "This is good leather work and might complement a fine cross."

"I found no other cord for the cross when I looked," Thomas said.

Eleanor went to the nun's side and stared at the loosened cord. It reminded her of the one Father Eliduc always wore around his own neck, then she chastised herself for wishing the body had been her nemesis and not Brother Gwydo. "Why did you say your judgment was faulty, Brother?"

"Adelard has his failings. He is rigid, arrogant, and spies on others to catch them in their sinning. I have found him lacking in compassion and charity."

"And yet?" Eleanor raised her eyebrow at the annoyance her monk made so evident.

"During the riot, when I told the villagers that the Church and its saints had forbidden violence against those of Jewish faith, he grew agitated." Thomas pressed his fingers against the bridge of his nose, trying to picture the scene more clearly. "He did not seem distraught because he believed I was lying to him but rather because he had never heard this prohibition before. I think he feared he had been in error about the condemnations he was advocating with such enthusiasm."

"Indeed?" Eleanor's eyes betrayed her amazement.

Sister Anne passed the cross to the crowner.

"And yet you found his cross near Brother Gwydo's body." Ralf fingered the loop on the top of the cross.

"Somehow I have misjudged the youth," Thomas replied, "but I am not sure whether I erred more in believing him capable of attacking those he called sinners or in thinking he might be converted to reason."

The prioress turned to the crowner. "Brother Gwydo has left the priory on a least one other occasion. On the day Kenelm was murdered, Adelard told Brother Thomas he had seen Gytha and our lay brother coupling."

Anne gasped. "That cannot be true. Those who take religious vows are not more chaste than she!"

The prioress waited.

Ralf stared at her in distressed silence.

She decided to lessen his misery. "He may well have seen them together, but he misinterpreted what he saw," she said. "Gytha had tumbled down the embankment on her way home from visiting her brother and hit her head. When she recovered her wits, the lay brother was beside her. He helped her to her feet and back to the priory."

"Other evidence I found before discovering the corpse would support her story," Thomas said. "When I took the shortcut to the village, I found a root that had been pulled up and signs that someone might have tripped and fallen over the side to the stream bank below. I went down to investigate, fearing our lay brother had been injured, but found no one."

"What Adelard must have seen is Brother Gwydo either kneeling by her side or helping her to her feet. She was dizzy and could not do so by herself." Eleanor spoke these words to the crowner.

"If the light was poor," he muttered. "Adelard might have misinterpreted that as an embrace. Since Brother Gwydo was a lay brother, he was not supposed to touch women."

"Well argued," Eleanor said gently.

"It was an act of compassion," Anne said.

"And not a violation of the spirit of his vows," Thomas added.

"Why would Adelard have killed Brother Gwydo or Kenelm?" Ralf tore his eyes away from the steady gaze of the prioress. "He is now the most likely suspect."

"He has established that he hated Master Jacob and his family for their faith and believes the blood libel and well-poisoning tales so common in the land," the prioress said. "To his mind, Kenelm sinned grievously by protecting those Adelard condemned. As for the death of Brother Gwydo, he may have decided to render his interpretation of God's justice because he believed the lay brother had broken his vows with my maid. For a religious to give in to lust is a profound wickedness." Eleanor gestured toward Thomas. "Finally, his cross has been found near our brother's corpse."

"If he is choosing to execute those whose behavior he finds most sinful, then our Gytha is in danger." Anne's face turned white. "Fool that Adelard is, he believes she lay with Brother Gwydo."

Eleanor spun around in horror.

"She must not leave your side, my lady," Ralf said, emotion cracking his voice.

Chapter Twenty-two

Jacob ben Asser knelt a short distance from Belia and cuddled their son in his arms. In this tiny stall they had little privacy with only a thick cloth over the door to keep the outside world away. Malka had just stepped outside to give the new parents time with their child, but she would not have wandered far. The riot had been quelled, but the danger of attack remained.

"You are worried," his wife said in a low voice.

"Have I ever been able to hide my thoughts from you?"

Belia smiled. "Even in childhood, we were one in both joy and sorrow."

"And we were fortunate that our families found our marriage to be of mutual benefit."

Belia whispered, "My mother always loved you like a son."

His eyebrows twitched upward. "You married me only to please your mother?"

She threw him a kiss.

He looked down at his sleeping son and watched silently as the boy blew bubbles from his mouth. "I would have lain down and died beside you had you not..."

Belia turned her face away. "The nun said I might not be able to bear more children," she murmured.

Shifting the precious burden into the crook of one arm, Jacob reached out to touch her cheek, then quickly drew back his hand. "Do not grieve," he said. "We have a fine son."

"Do not say it! Our boy is a poor thing, ugly and ill-natured. To say otherwise is to tempt evil things."

"Very well," he replied, frowning at the child with difficulty. "Then it is well if you are unable to bear more for this creature will shame me. It seems I must also suffer the grief of having you at my side for the rest of my life." He could jest no further and he bent as close as he dared. "I love you," he whispered.

"You need other children, Jacob. Divorce me. Marry a woman with a fruitful womb. My mother would grieve but not stop you."

"As your husband, I may order you to do as I wish, a right I have never exercised. Now I must and so decree that you shall never again speak of this. I have no wish to marry another. If it is meet, you may bear us more children as Sarah did in her old age to Abraham, but I will not cast you aside for another. As I was named Jacob, so are you my Rachel."

"Then you are a fool, beloved."

"And hence you exceeded all other women in pious compassion when you wedded me without protest."

They laughed and, for a long moment, said nothing more but took comfort in watching their son innocently dream.

"Yet you are still troubled," Belia said again. "If the reason is not my future barrenness, or the health of either your son or wife, what causes that shadow to drift across your eyes?"

"We cannot remain in England. I want our child to grow up in a land where he may laugh and find joy without fear."

"My mother would say that our people will never find such a land until the *mashiach* leads us back to Jerusalem and our Temple is rebuilt."

"A time we may never live to see," he said, his brow furrowed, "but we shall make plans after our return to Norwich. Others are less fortunate than we and have little means to escape. You have an uncle in Avignon who speaks well of the conditions there, although the quarter allowed us is crowded. I have merchant cousins who claim that Fez is a safer place. Finding a new home may be hard, but I have skills to start a new life. We had already agreed that this new king has taken too much with nothing given in return."

She pressed a hand to her heart. "I feel a greater sorrow yet in you." Taking a deep breath, she continued. "I know more than you realize about what happened. Now that my trials are over, there is nothing you need keep from me."

Jacob tilted his head back toward the stall entrance. "He has not come back."

"Did he say he would?"

The babe grew restless in his arms and began to whimper.

The curtain flew back and Malka rushed in. Taking the child from Jacob, she placed him into her daughter's open arms. "He is ready to nurse," she said, "and you are forbidden to touch your wife."

Her son-in-law looked at her, his expression shifting from annoyance to gratitude.

"I listen only for the needs of my grandchild," Malka said, holding her twisted hands to her ears. "Therefore speak softly when you compliment me." She smiled and retreated to the stall entrance. Turning briefly, she added, "Otherwise, I shall wait to be summoned."

"Your heart will tell you of any need even if your ears do not," he replied, the words fondly spoken.

His mother-in-law laughed and left them alone.

Belia put the babe to her breast, her face glowing.

"Our son is a lusty eater," her husband said in amazement.

"Just like his father," Belia replied with a twinkle in her eye.

In awe the parents watched until the child had suckled, belched, and fallen back asleep.

"Continue your story," his wife said.

Jacob shifted to rest his back against the stall. "He and I were like brothers when we were children. I went to his house and he to mine. On baking day, ours was the most popular place to meet. Until she died, my mother gave all the children sweets."

"But boys become men, and the difference in faith builds walls between us as it did with that poor boy, William, in

Norwich. We were cruelly condemned for killing a child our mothers welcomed and fed."

"Would that boys never become men if hate is the result." There was sorrow in his voice.

"You should be grateful the man you considered a brother did not stab you to death when you last met. Did he not threaten to kill you once before?"

He looked upon his sleeping son, and tears glistened in the corner of his eyes. "He did, swearing to slit my throat if I did not forsake my faith for his. I refused, saying that no man respects another who breaks an oath, even one deemed in error. So how could Christians not look at a man with suspicion and doubt if he abandons his faith to follow another? Is that not an oath broken? There is no safety for us in that choice, and those who convert often suffer much grief."

"Do you truly believe he means now to make peace with you?"

"Not all Christians in this land hold us in contempt."

"My mother would concur and refuses to praise or condemn any, whether Jewish or Christian, on the basis of faith alone. But dare you believe that this man, who once held his knife to your throat, has changed his mind?"

"He did not kill me then either."

"Only because my mother walked into the courtyard and reminded him that murder was against every law, a rule honored by all good men."

"He does now beg forgiveness for what he did."

"Then seek my mother's advice on what you should do. She rarely errs in judging men's hearts. Did she not allow a nun to help me give birth to our child?"

"She knew the nun's father in Norwich, a physician and one whom she and your father both respected."

"Despite my birth pains, I heard them talking as if there was no difference between them. Since my mother can look beyond the symbols of faith, she will tell you honestly if she questions the sincerity of your boyhood friend."

Jacob nodded in the direction of the absent mother-in-law. "Your mother did know him when he was a child. I shall listen to her opinion and shall seek it again about what we should plan to do after we are safely in Norwich."

"My mother has learned to survive the vagaries of Christian tolerance. In this kingdom, we once knew kindness from King Henry II. Even the late king, Henry III, took our part in court, but his son finds persecution more profitable. I agree with her that we shall always be guests in any realm. Even if we travel to the Great Sea and seek asylum in the land of Hagar's descendants, we must never forget that the welcome offered is only for a brief time." Her voice dulled with growing fatigue.

He looked over his shoulder at the entrance to their tiny shelter. "Meanwhile, a lay brother from the priory stands outside to keep the villagers from killing us, that at the order of a prioress."

"My mother finds members of this priory to be honorable and kind. Of all the villagers, the innkeeper came to comfort me in my travail." She smiled at him. "You know that my mother seeks the true nature of any mortal in the eyes' light. Did I not follow her teaching and discover how loving you were?" Then she gazed at the tiny child at her breast. "And see what a gift you gave me!"

Jacob flushed, and then rose to his feet. "I must let you rest," he said, "and send in your mother to lie near you while you sleep. It must be safe to take a short walk between inn and stables. When I return, I shall bed down in the next stall." He kissed his fingers and directed them to his wife. "As you said, our hearts are never apart even when I must keep my distance until your *mikveh*."

"And surely I can take the ritual bath soon after we arrive in Norwich," she murmured, her eyes closing against her will with weariness.

He watched her fall asleep, the babe still snuggled against her breast, then pulled aside the cloth and stepped outside the stall.

Malka rose to her feet, nodding at the sleeping maid in the straw, and gestured for Jacob to leave the stables with her. "Of course, I cannot be sure that you would ever seek my opinion on such a matter, but I was just thinking that your friend seemed truly repentant when he last approached you," she said in a low voice.

He smiled at her phrasing and thanked her. Then they stood for a long time, staring in silence at the rigid back of Brother Beorn.

"Fez, I think," she said softly. "I have heard that the emir was outraged at the recent violence against us there and promised protection if we bring our skills and learning to serve him. All who do not share his faith, whether Christian or Jew, must surely pay a fine and give their oath that they will not attempt to convert any from the faith practiced in that land. The oath is reasonable, and any fines no worse than we would suffer elsewhere."

Jacob kissed her cheek. "You did say that you heard only what pertained to your grandson," he said with a chuckle. "He shall learn Arabic then."

She nodded. "Another language, added to the several we already know, is useful in business and in the courts of rulers." She turned around and reached for the cloth covering the entrance. "'Tis a pity she must wait to be cleansed until we return to Norwich, but that will give her more time to heal."

"I would do nothing to endanger her health," Jacob replied, pulling the heavy cloth back for her.

"That is one of the many reasons I am grateful you married my daughter," she said and disappeared into the stables.

Jacob shut his eyes but knew he could not sleep. The night was soft. The heat of the day lingered with the sweet scent of warm flowers, and there was a hint of moisture in the air that presaged rain. In that moment, he felt at peace. His wife was growing stronger. His son cried lustily and fed like a lion cub. Perhaps the worst had passed?

He walked deeper into the darkness.

Chapter Twenty-three

Ralf slammed the leather jack on the scarred table and swung his hand in the approximate direction of the ale jug.

"It is empty, my lord." Cuthbert grabbed the object out of harm's way and gestured to the serving wench for another.

"I cannot even get properly drunk." Ralf's snarl exploded into a loud belch.

Raising an eyebrow, the sergeant chose not to contradict the man whom he served.

It took only a moment for the woman to slide a freshly filled jug across the table toward the two men. She glanced at Cuthbert's almost full jack and the crowner's dry one. "Compliments of Mistress Signy," she said and marched off.

"Now that wench would be a fine mare to ride through the night. Look how those hips sway!" Ralf's leer was decidedly askew.

The sergeant shrugged.

Ralf ran a palm over the stubble on his face. He was growing morose. In truth, his manhood might hope the woman would follow him to the hayloft, but the rest of his body wanted to go home to a beloved wife. And if not tonight, tomorrow he would have preferred to remain sober.

He pushed the heels of his hands into his eyes and groaned. The only wife he longed to have waiting for him was Gytha, a woman whom he had insulted beyond all hope of forgiveness.

He banged his fist on the table and cursed.

Cuthbert slid a bit further down the bench.

"A lifetime of friendship with Tostig," the crowner mumbled, then realized he had spoken aloud. And years of an evolving love for Gytha herself, he said to himself. All destroyed in a few moments of blind stupidity. Had he ever known her to lie? Why had he not taken her word at once? He let loose a stream of creative profanity.

Cuthbert sighed and drank a small amount of his own ale. This promised to be a long night. Despite what he had suggested when the crowner asked him to guard the Jewish family, his wife was lovingly patient. Had it not been for Ralf's benevolence, they could never have married, a fact which allowed for a prolonged time of gratitude.

A burst of laughter rolled through the inn. In one corner a man was shouting the words to a lewd song. Just to their left, another got up on the table and began a rocky but enthusiastic dance.

"I cannot tolerate this!" Ralf hissed.

Cuthbert looked at him in surprise. The crowner now seemed unaccountably sober. "A miracle," he murmured and stared at his own drink in case he had forgotten how much he had drunk himself.

"I need air," Ralf said. "If the king wants to write new laws, let him forbid levity when I'm suffering." Sliding along the length of the bench, he pushed Cuthbert in front of him, leapt to his feet, and headed for the door.

Signy waved to the crowner as he passed, then turned to the long-suffering sergeant who followed. "An attack of black or yellow bile?" she asked.

"Black as Satan's ass," he grumbled, then gave her a weak smile in response to her sympathetic tone.

"Tell him that Sister Anne should apply a leech to his pintle. That will surely cure him!"

"I dare not," Cuthbert said with a laugh.

"I do." Signy smiled and walked away.

◇◇◇

Outside, the crowner slowed his pace and turned toward the new stables.

Brother Beorn looked up when Ralf approached. His expression was not welcoming.

The crowner stopped and nodded.

The lay brother grunted and folded his arms.

Although Beorn was surely unhappy that his prioress had sent him to guard a Jewish family, Ralf saw that he had obeyed with his usual diligence. That thin-shanked, beetle-eyed religious could scare the Devil himself, and it was well the man had been assigned to watch during Satan's hours of darkness. In truth, that was a compliment, for Ralf felt no more love for Brother Beorn than the lay brother did for him. Resentments spawned in their boyhood had not faded.

"You are a far better guard than Kenelm, even with his cudgel," Ralf muttered. "That look is fierce enough to frighten away any mortal with sense."

Beorn's expression took on a surprised hue.

"I need to piss," the crowner said and strode off.

Cuthbert raised a hand in greeting to the lay brother and followed his superior at a courteous distance.

◇◇◇

When Ralf turned the corner of the partially constructed stables, he stopped, momentarily unsure of where to walk. Clouds had swiftly covered the moon and chased away the brighter light. Blinking to clear his vision, he thought he saw something move in the darkness.

He squinted. Was that a man running away? Perhaps it was only a shadow changing shape as the clouds dimmed the moonlight.

Standing still, he listened, but a burst of laughter and tuneless singing from the inn overpowered any sound of footsteps. He must have been wrong, he decided, and, his eyes now better accustomed to the darkness, he continued on to find a place to relieve himself.

Suddenly, just a few yards in front of him, a man leapt from the ground and cried out.

"What has happened here?" Ralf drew his sword and rushed forward.

As if commanded, the moonlight brightened with a sickly glow.

The man standing was Jacob ben Asser. The body at his feet was that of Adelard.

"Cuthbert!" Ralf pushed ben Asser back against the stable wall and rested the point of his sword against the man's chest.

The sergeant came running.

As he gave orders to his subordinate, the crowner did not take his eyes from his captive. "We have a corpse. Tell Mistress Signy we need sober men to carry it to the priory hospital. Prioress Eleanor must be informed by one of those men. We shall beg her permission to let Sister Anne take charge of it. You will summon Tostig. I need him to house and guard this suspect."

Jacob opened his mouth but nothing came out.

Cuthbert spun around and left.

"I am arresting you for the murder of the baker's son," Ralf said to his captive.

"I am innocent!" Jacob's eyes looked white with terror even in the weak moonlight.

The crowner grabbed his shoulder and held him firmly. Feeling the man tremble, Ralf sheathed his sword. It was unlikely ben Asser would try to escape or attack, and he felt an odd twinge of sorrow.

Jacob tried to gesture in the direction of the stable. "Whatever crime you wish to lay on my head, my family is innocent. A newborn babe and three women can do no ill to anyone, and they are helpless against those who wish them harm. Have mercy on us or at least have compassion for my family!"

"I am doing that," Ralf growled. "Your family will remain under the protection of the priory, but no one can guarantee their safety if I do not take you into custody for this death. You may be innocent of all wrong, but the village does not care.

They have already condemned you for Kenelm's murder." He gestured at Adelard's body. "Your guard's body may have been found some distance away, but this corpse lies at your very door."

Chapter Twenty-four

Adelard blinked. Shadows swirled around him like smoke. "Am I in Heaven?" he murmured, but the words echoed in his ears as if he were standing on the edge of an abyss. One vague form bent closer, and he grew frightened. "Or have my sins sent me to Hell?"

Prioress Eleanor stepped into a flickering pale ray of candlelight. "Neither. You are in the hospital at Tyndal Priory."

"Are you sure?" the youth asked, wondering at the halo of light around this woman who spoke. Then Sister Christina rose from her knees and laid a hand on his forehead. Her expression was beatifically vague. He gasped and drew the sheet closer around his neck. "An angel!"

Stirring something in a tan pottery bowl, Sister Anne walked up to the bed. "Our infirmarian's prayers have surely wrought a miracle. We thought you were dead when the men carried you here."

Sister Christina stepped away, silently bowed to her prioress, and left. Her footsteps were so light that it was doubtful her feet ever touched the dusty earth.

Sister Anne glanced fondly at her retreating, near-sighted and gentle superior, then turned around to pour her potion into a small mazer. Sniffing at it to confirm potency, she brought it close to Adelard's lips. "Drink," she said. "It is bitter but will ease your pain."

Squeezing his eyes shut, Adelard dutifully swallowed. Despite being told that the vision he had just seen was not an angel, he was convinced she was at least a saint, and thus he grew inclined to obedience.

"Are you able to answer questions?"

The deep voice came from somewhere the youth could not see, and his body visibly jerked with fright.

Eleanor looked at Ralf and gestured for him to come where the young man could see him.

Adelard seemed relieved that the voice was a mortal one, but his expression still suggested that he saw little difference between an imp and this king's man. "I will try to do so, my lord."

"Why did you go to the stables?" Ralf's voice was rough with impatience.

"I went to pray for the souls of the Jews." He began to tremble again. "I did not mean to trouble their sleep, my lord. I know you sent me back to my father the last time you saw me there, but I swear that these prayers were to be quiet ones."

"Did Brother Beorn see you?"

"He did and queried me about my purpose. When I told him that I wished to pray for their conversions, he nodded approval but asked if I had any weapon. I gave him my eating knife. He let me pass."

"Odd that the toad never said anything to me about this," Ralf muttered, then continued: "Where did you go?"

"The back of the stables. I did not want anyone else to see me."

At least Adelard had been found where he claimed to have gone. Ralf told the young man to continue.

"I knelt near the wall and began to beseech God to change the hearts of these infidels. I had only begun when I felt a sharp pain. Then I remember nothing more."

"Were you kneeling when you were attacked?"

"Yes, my lord."

Ralf grunted and glanced at Sister Anne.

"The nature of his head wound suggests he tells the truth," she said.

"I would not lie!" Adelard gestured around him. "I am in God's house. To say aught but the truth would condemn my soul."

The crowner opened his mouth, but one glance from Sister Anne was enough for him to shut it instantly. She knew him too well, and this was neither the time nor place for his retort that lies were spoken here as well as on secular lands.

"I swear I had not been there long before I was struck." Adelard looked away.

Eleanor noticed the gesture and looked over her shoulder at Brother Thomas standing quietly behind her. She tilted her head toward the youth.

He nodded, indicating that he, too, suspected the baker's son had more to say but also had some reason to hesitate.

"What do you recall before the blow? I want to know everything: shadows, smells, sounds." Ralf raised his hand. "And swear that you shall tell the truth as God demands."

Brother Thomas moved into the youth's line of vision and gave him the comfort of a blessing.

"But what if I say something that points to blame in the wrong direction? Is that not a sin?" Adelard addressed this to Brother Thomas.

"You must reveal all that you can," the monk replied. "From that, Crowner Ralf shall weave your memories into a tapestry of truth."

The young man scowled with evident worry and fell silent.

"Did the Jew strike you?" Ralf bent down until his nose almost touched that of the young man.

Tears began to run down the sides of Adelard's face.

Sister Anne cleared her throat. "Enough, Ralf. The youth suffers from his wound and needs rest. Come back when he has slept and regained at least a little strength. Surely there is nothing more you can do until after the sun rises." She looked up at the gray color in one of the nearby windows. "That will be soon enough."

The crowner threw his hands up in disgust and strode away.

As he passed Thomas, the monk grasped his arm. "Let us walk a short way together," he said and then whispered something into the crowner's ear.

Ralf stopped and turned back to look at Adelard. In the deeper shadows, the crowner's expression was softer as he addressed the wounded young man. "I seek only the truth and do not want to hang a man who is not guilty. But I am still the crown's representative, and King Edward's law must be upheld. However, if something troubles your soul…" He waited for a response.

Adelard stared back hopefully.

"Brother Thomas is here to offer advice and succor," Ralf continued. Although he did little to disguise his annoyance with this delay, the crowner managed to convey some kindness. "I can wait. After you have spoken with the good monk, you may feel able to add more details to what you said this night."

"I thank you," Adelard whispered. "I would speak with Brother Thomas, for I need his wisdom in order to recover my spiritual strength."

Ralf bowed to the monk and smiled but there was no mockery in that. Usually he agreed with this prioress and her monk, although he saw some danger in their current stratagem. Nonetheless, the method was clever if it worked. He spun on his heel and left.

Prioress Eleanor followed, keeping a short distance behind him as they walked between the rows of sick and dying. One woman in great pain begged for a blessing to help her endure the struggle. Next, the prioress stopped to kneel beside Brother John, who was comforting a man fighting to draw in his last earthly breath.

When she emerged into the courtyard, she looked around, fearing the crowner had left the priory, but then she saw him leaning against the wall and waiting. Eleanor approached and bent her head back to look up at him. "What do you think now about the baker's son?"

"He is no longer the primary suspect," he said, "although the discovery of that cross near Brother Gwydo's corpse must be explained. The youth's moral condemnations in the past may have smelled rank to many noses, but, since the Jewish family became his target, the village would deem those rants as fragrant as a lily. I doubt anyone except our killer is the one who did this. Adelard must have seen something."

"And he cannot have struck such a blow to the back of his own head any more than Brother Gwydo could have strangled himself."

"Nor do I like Jacob ben Asser for the killer." He scratched his back against the rough stones.

"As we previously discussed, he could not have killed our lay brother. If Adelard did pray quietly, as he claims, and did nothing else to molest the family, what reason would the new father have for striking the youth?"

"Had ben Asser not leapt up and called out to me, I might not have seen him kneeling beside the youth. Guilty men do strange things, but few deliberately bring unwanted attention to themselves." He rubbed his aching eyes. "It was dark. He could have slipped away."

"Brother Thomas has said that he seems a good man, which makes his refusal to seek conversion all the more tragic." Eleanor shook her head. "We shall continue to hope for that, but I agree that Jacob ben Asser is not a likely murderer."

"So we are left with no suspects." He tried to smile. "At least there is one good that has come out of this crime tonight. We feared Adelard was killing those he believed to have sinned. Since he has become a victim himself, Mistress Gytha is no longer in danger."

"She will be pleased to hear that. She longs to visit her brother, as is her wont."

"There seems no reason to deny her wish."

"And what of the Jewish family?"

"I have put Jacob ben Asser in Tostig's custody until this matter is settled. Should any man approach that house with ill intent, Tostig will break his head. Ben Asser is safe there, but he worries that his family is without defense. I tried to convince him that his arrest would forestall any violence, but I am not so confident."

"Then the priory will guarantee it. Brother Beorn is now on guard near the family's door. At day break, I will send strong, young lay brothers with stout cudgels to relieve him. Prior Andrew will gather the villagers together so they may hear the news of the arrest before they begin labors, and he shall make it clear that this priory supports the king's right to render proper justice. Anyone who lays one finger on any member of ben Asser's guiltless family will suffer the Church's condemnation as well as King Edward's." Her eyes narrowed. "Few would imperil both their souls and their necks."

Although Ralf doubted that any would actually be excommunicated in this situation, he believed the threat was enough to keep men with pitchforks from howling for the blood of helpless women and their babe. Unless the killer was found quickly, however, even Tostig and Prioress Eleanor could not stop the slaughter of innocents.

"And what shall you do now, Ralf?" Her tone softened as she looked at the weary and sorrowful man.

"Let Brother Thomas calm Adelard so he will answer my questions when he awakens after taking Annie's sleeping potion. I am hoping he has seen something that will lead us to the killer of both your lay brother and Kenelm. Were I to guess at the meaning of the attack on the baker's son, I would say that Jacob ben Asser may have saved the boy's life by appearing before another blow was struck. In the dark, I had the impression I had seen someone run away."

"The youth has much to learn, but our good monk believes there may be some hope for him. Brother Thomas will do his best to encourage him to cooperate with you." She looked kindly at the crowner. "And will you seek your bed as well, Ralf?"

He bowed. "I shall go question my prisoner. Since he is of the Jewish faith, he may not claim the right to confess his sins to a priest and keep them private." His lips twisted into a thin smile. "Since I seek a murderer, I am most grateful for that."

Chapter Twenty-five

Tostig reached for a thick iron rod when he heard the sound of someone at the door.

Ralf stopped in the entrance and raised his hands. "A friend!"

Putting his weapon down, Gytha's brother invited the crowner to join him.

"Drinking with the prisoner?" Ralf stared at Jacob sitting on a bench with a mazer of ale in his hand.

Tostig raised a jug and gestured to an empty cup.

"My throat is dry enough. I would be grateful for that." Ralf walked over and took the proffered cup for his friend to fill. Drinking deeply, he turned back to the seated man.

Even as the pale light of early morning strengthened, Jacob's face lacked color. "My family?"

"They are well," Ralf said. "Prioress Eleanor has sent to the stable several young lay brothers with strength aplenty and permission enough to break bones. But, as I heard her tell it, their faces are so angelic that villagers might pause before throwing rocks at them lest they be true messengers from God."

"Your prioress has been kind."

"She believes in the perfection of God's justice and has little tolerance for flawed mortal judgments." He slid onto the bench across the table from Jacob. "If you are innocent, she will protect you. If not, she'll beg me to hang you."

"There is more ale there," Tostig said, pointing to a corner of the house. "Above you, out of the way of mice, are bread and cheese to break your fast. I'll walk to the inn for some of Mistress Signy's fare and listen for the latest rumors on these crimes." He slapped the crowner on the shoulder. "I may even tell you what I learn." Then he grinned and left.

"He has been a kind jailor." Jacob ran his mazer around in a circle on the table.

"Not all Christians own horns and forked tails."

The man smiled briefly, but the weight of his situation lay too heavily on his heart for true levity.

"I have oft wondered if you portray us the way we depict you."

Jacob stiffened with wariness. "Do you think we would so brazenly mock Christians, an act for which we would surely be punished, when we are set on fire, beaten, and hanged for crimes we have not committed?"

Ralf retrieved the suspended food and brought it back to the table. "Not openly, but all men try to shine with virtue in the world. In private, their deeds are more rank." He pulled out his knife and hacked slices of both bread and cheese, pushing some toward Jacob. He paused. "Your religion forbids so much. Dare you eat here?"

Jacob's lips twitched briefly. "I am not required to starve to death in extreme situations, but the good innkeeper has provided us with fish from the stream, fresh summer fruits and vegetables so we might prepare them in accordance with our law. While I am in this house, Tostig will allow our maid to bring me food cooked in our own pot." Looking at the proffered cheese and bread, he thanked the crowner for his kindness and gently refused.

Ralf hesitated and then shrugged. "Are you truly innocent of any crime since you came to Tyndal village?"

"No simple aye or nay would be an adequate reply. May I answer in my own way?"

The crowner nodded and bit into the moist cheese.

"Why would I kill the very guard set by the innkeeper to protect us? And, having seen how the men of this village reacted to that man's death, why would I kill the young man I found outside our shelter?" He took a sip from his cup. "My wife was heavy with child when we arrived. Later, she delivered after a hard labor, a birth that almost killed her. We cannot leave until she gains strength. Would I be so foolish as to kill two men in such circumstances and endanger those I cherish more than my own life?"

"The village concludes that you have killed Kenelm and, when they learn of it, will decide the same about Adelard."

"The village believes I killed the guard simply because he was a Christian. Presumably, they will think I killed the youth because we failed to convert when he demanded we do so." Jacob threw his hands up in disgust. "Crowner, we do not poison wells. We do not use Christian blood for Passover baking. It is my people who have died by Christian swords, not the reverse. Since truth has been murdered by ignorance and justice blinded by sanctified hate, how can any of us defend ourselves?" He shook his head. "And I should have said none of that to you, but I am weary of having to cut myself again and again to prove that I bleed like any other man."

Ralf poured ale into the man's cup. "It matters not whether I dislike you for your beliefs. It is my duty to render justice whether or not I like a man. I have hanged Christians, found guilty of great crimes, with whom I might otherwise have shared a jug of ale. As Crowner, I take no joy in watching a man strangle on a rope for a wrong he did not commit."

Jacob nodded.

"So tell me all that you know about the deaths of your guard and the baker's son. If you are guilty, confess it. I shall then take you to the gallows, but on my oath as a man born of an honorable father, I promise that your family will be safely returned to Norwich. If you are innocent, you shall go with them."

"Then ask what you need to know, and that may freshen my memory. I swear I am innocent of disobeying the commandment we all honor, but I shall reply honestly." Jacob drained his mazer.

Ralf poured more for both of them. "Let us begin with Kenelm. He mocked you. You did strike him in anger. Perhaps

he died by accident and you wished to hide the deed, not trusting the rule of law here."

"I could not have killed him. As I told you, my wife was weak
and suffering before she gave birth. I did not leave her side. Sadly,
the only witnesses for the entire time are my wife, her mother,
and perhaps our servant who is barely more than a child." He
thought for a moment. "The innkeeper did visit several times.
She feared she might have to be midwife." He glanced down at
his mazer and grew pensive.

Ralf watched him, waited, and then lost patience. "You have
something to say. If you want to hang before your babe leaves
his mother's breast, then remain silent." He leaned forward.
"But while you decide how much you dare trust me with any
confidence, remember this. A nun saved your wife and child.
A prioress has sent her lay brothers to guard your family from
riots. A king's man has given his word to return your kin, alive
and well, to the safety of Norwich even if you do hang. Is that
not the kind of justice you seek?"

"And what if the truth were to cast a shadow on your priory?
Would a Christian take the word of a Jew or is it more likely
that I would be condemned simply because I dared speak of it?"

"Prioress Eleanor does not turn her face from unhappy
truths. I will judge the meaning of what you claim." Ralf knew
he had spoken firmly, but he clutched his hands together lest
they tremble.

"The night of Kenelm's death, the man you know as Brother
Gwydo came to visit me."

Ralf's mouth dropped open. "Why?"

"He and I were boyhood friends in Cambridge. Then a bishop
came and preached the call to save Jerusalem from those he condemned as infidels. The burning brand of his words lit a fire in
Gwydo's heart and he turned from me, for I was not of his faith.
He demanded I accept his beliefs. I refused, saying that we had
suffered too much from the cruelty of Christians to believe they
were the new chosen people of *The Merciful One*. We fought.
He would have slit my throat, had another not saved me, and

then he left. His last words were that I must accept baptism or he would kill me on his return with a sword red with the blood of other unbelievers."

The crowner's jaw tightened. "I am no priest and have no wish to debate God's favor. Keep your tale simple."

"He went on his pilgrimage but did not return even when King Edward came back. I heard a rumor that his father and wife were mourning him so assumed he must be dead." Jacob sighed. "The night of the guard's death, however, someone tapped on the entrance to our stall. Thinking it might be the innkeeper, I pulled aside the curtain, but it was a man. He was tonsured. Suddenly, he fell to his knees and wept. Confused, I drew back, but I heard a tone of voice, saw a familiar gesture, and recognized my former friend. We embraced, my tears joining his, and he begged forgiveness for his cruelty to me. I did not ask how he learned I had come to this village. That detail meant so little."

"To leave the priory without permission is not allowed," was all Ralf managed to say.

"We sat outside the stall and talked. He told me why he had changed. Even when men kill for a cause deemed holy, he said, they sin grievously. He learned to abhor violence of all kinds and came to believe that one must never kill another man. The lesson of Cain and Abel is that we are all brothers. He had retreated to a priory as penance and begged me to keep his secret, for he had truly forsaken the world."

"How long was he with you?"

"I do not know exactly when your Brother Gwydo left to return to the priory, but it had grown dark. Still, he is witness to my presence here for some time." Jacob ran a finger under his eyes. "But if speaking on my behalf would bring him punishment for an act of gentle kindness, I would rather he not be questioned."

Sitting back, Ralf thought for a moment. "He might have killed Kenelm on his way back to the priory. Did he have any reason to do so? Or perhaps the guard saw him and threatened to tell Prioress Eleanor?"

Jacob gasped. "The man with whom I reconciled that night was no longer one who could do such a thing! Perhaps his disobedience in leaving the priory is deemed a sin, but his intent was to seek forgiveness. Nor has he repeated this act. Surely your prioress, one who has offered protection to a helpless family, would not treat him harshly, and surely she knows him well enough to agree that he is a gentle man."

"Brother Gwydo will never suffer," the crowner said. "He is dead."

Jacob rose to his feet in horror. "How? What plague has struck him down? Or did he die at the same hands as the one who killed the guard?"

The crowner grabbed the man's robe and pulled him back down on the bench. "For the sake of your friend, if not yourself, you must not hold back anything more. The one who killed him surely murdered Kenelm and Adelard."

"There is nothing else I can tell you," Jacob said, his voice rough with tears. "After we had spoken of his life in Outremer and mine in Cambridge, he left. I went back into the stall. My wife, our young maid, and my mother-in-law had fallen asleep, but I could not. I sat until dawn and watched over them."

"Might Gwydo have known Kenelm in Cambridge?"

"The guard came from the north, or so he claimed. And he was never in Jerusalem. He once said he had not taken the cross. Perhaps that was why he mocked us so cruelly."

"Tell me about finding Adelard." Ralf considered drinking what was left in the jug but pushed his cup aside.

"My wife and I had been talking about our son and our future after we return to Norwich. When she grew weary, I left her to sleep, but I was too restless and went into the courtyard for a short walk."

"Did you see Brother Beorn?"

Jacob nodded. "The man glared at me." Glancing at the crowner, he smiled briefly. "For that, I should be grateful. At least he can confirm when I left."

"Then?"

"I walked behind the stables, away from the guard's view. Suddenly, I stopped, thinking I had seen someone running away. Perhaps the one shadow had been a pair, lovers seeking a quiet moment together and whom I had frightened. But the moon was shrouded, and I could confirm nothing in fact. I decided I had imagined it all, but when I turned to walk on, I stumbled."

"Aye?"

"I fell on something and feared it was a body. Terrified at what that might mean, I rolled away and got to my knees. When I felt around, I knew the shape was that of a man, one who lay quite still."

"Why did you not shout for help? Brother Beorn was near."

"Because I heard voices. I recognized yours and called for aid."

Ralf reconsidered the contents of the jug and poured himself a last mazer of ale. "So you thought you saw someone fleeing before you tripped. There may have been a witness after all, or else a killer," he muttered. "I need only find a shadow."

"And the lad? How did he die? I pray he did not suffer."

"You should have been able to tell something from the position of the stab wound."

"I did not feel for any wound," Jacob snapped, "and it was too dark to see."

"What weapons do you own?"

"My kind jailor asked the same. I gave him my small table knife which he has hidden away. Ask him for it. You may check for blood and, if you think I cleaned it before you arrested me, I wear the same clothes now." He stood. "Do you wish to look for stains?"

Ralf shook his head.

"As for any other weapon, I carry nothing else."

"Then breath more easily," Ralf said. "The lad who troubled your wife's rest with his loud preaching will live."

Jacob ben Asser covered his face with his hands and murmured a prayer of thanks.

Ralf, on the other hand, stared upward with less gratitude. He no longer had any good suspects but too many dead bodies.

Chapter Twenty-six

Thomas did not like Adelard, but his heart softened when he saw the fear in the lad's eyes. Many would say that the baker's son was ready to take on the burdens of manhood along with a man's beard, but there was a quivering child reflected in the gaze of this youth of eighteen summers. "I offer solace and guidance," the monk said. The gentleness in his voice was sincere.

"My heart is heavy, Brother. Crimes oppress my soul. I must have your counsel." Adelard's words tumbled out in a rush.

"That I shall give, but you must speak the truth. Whatever sins have been committed, your soul is of greater worth than your body. Do you swear you shall be honest, whatever the consequences?"

"I do." The youth looked away. "But I could not speak to the crowner until I was clear on what must be spoken and what might be left in silence." His words were muffled. "Ask what you will, then guide me."

Thomas decided it was kinder to begin with an event that had not led to a death. "Why were you by the stables?"

"I did not lie when I said I wished to pray for the Jews' conversion, but there was another reason. I hoped God would take pity on me in the solitude of darkness if I continued to beg for enlightenment after your revelations."

Thomas was pleased. Adelard's troubled reaction to the news that Pope Gregory himself rejected the mythical condemnations against those of Jewish faith spoke well of the youth. "What do you recall of the attack?"

"Nothing!"

The response was too swift and the young man's nervous pitch suggested he was hiding something despite his oath. The monk waited, but Adelard offered nothing more. Very well, Thomas said to himself, if he refuses to answer an easy question, I shall ask harder ones. "What happened to the silver cross you always wear?"

Adelard paled and began to tremble.

This time Thomas showed no pity. "Lest your soul burn in Hell, keep your word and tell the truth."

"I lost it the day of the riot. My father saw it was missing and berated me, but I have neither found it nor heard that anyone else did."

Thomas saw nothing in the youth's demeanor to suggest he was lying. Although inclined to believe him, the monk knew that made the problem of why the cross was found near Gwydo's body all the more confusing. "When did you first notice it was gone?"

"After the riot, I left the village for the seclusion of the forest. Your words to the men of Tyndal village distressed my soul. When I returned later, my father saw that I no longer wore it. I have since searched for it diligently but to no avail." Tears collected in the corners of his eyes.

"Where did you go in the forest?" This news did not bode well for the youth's innocence.

"Please, Brother! I would answer your questions, but my spirit is tortured. Out of compassion for this great sinner, will you first ease my pain?" The tears now flowed like a deluge.

The answer to the question of location was crucial to determining if the youth had been near where the body of Gwydo had been found, but Thomas' role as priest demanded precedence. "Is it confession you wish?"

"I need understanding first," Adelard whispered. "Then I may better cleanse my soul of all its foulness. And I swear to undertake whatever penance you require."

"Ask your questions freely for I never condemn any seeker of truth." As much as he longed to continue the pursuit of information, he knew he must honor a soul's hunger before all else. If he gave the comfort he swore he would offer, he was also more likely to get the youth's cooperation. That thought brought him the patience required to continue.

"We are commanded to obey and honor our parents, yet we are expected to leave them to follow our Lord. I do not understand the contradiction."

Since he was a bastard and his own mother had died too early in his life, Thomas had never considered this question in any depth. Clearing his throat to give himself time to think, he still failed to come up with a satisfactory reply. "What has caused you to be troubled by this?"

"In the matter of the Jews, my father taught me to hate them. Yet you say both popes and saints require mercy and tolerance."

"I have already quoted the substance of those commands. Although we may grieve that their conversion is slow, we may not give in to intolerance. According to the teachings of Saint Paul, who was himself an Israelite, Israel shall be saved only when all Gentiles are converted." Must he repeat his entire sermon to the rioters? Thomas tried not to show his annoyance.

Adelard's forehead wrinkled in thought.

"Perhaps your father was not aware of these words," Thomas said.

"The priest who taught him believed otherwise."

Raising an eyebrow, Thomas was struck again with a suspicion he had had earlier. "Did your father once hope to take vows himself?"

"He had learned some Latin, but his father was a poor man and did not have the means to buy him a position in a monastery." Adelard rubbed moisture from his cheeks. "Nor could he banish lust," he said, "and thus married my mother, but she was a woman of deep faith who turned to prayer and celibacy after bearing my youngest brother."

"Does your own longing to take vows come from your father's heart or from your own?" Thomas was not sure where this was leading, but at least he might be able answer whether Adelard should become a novice. This young man had the choice of staying in the world and practicing an honorable trade. If the passion for God was borrowed, he ought to remain a baker. Maybe he could be encouraged to contribute to the keep of those who, like his father, were unable to pay for a place in God's house…

Adelard tilted his head, and then winced for the gesture caused him pain. "It was always my father's greatest wish, one that I would not deny him, but I have come to long for it myself."

Thomas was not so sure, but he was finally ready to answer the youth's uncertainty about obedience. "Then you are learning the answer to your initial question, my son," he said. "We must honor our parents, a true commandment, but the seeking for truth must come from our own hearts. Sometimes that means finding wisdom they lack."

"Please explain, Brother."

"As an example, I shall speak of the matter regarding the Jews. Remember that God forbade the worship of other gods? To take hate into your heart, when He has ordered it to be the house of love, is to worship Satan. The Prince of Darkness is the deity of hate." Thomas took a deep breath and hoped he had made sense.

The baker's son looked at him with amazement.

"But I do not mean to disparage all your father has taught you, for he must have sought the truth himself as a youth." Thomas remembered the large, ruddy-faced man with tiny eyes and had difficulty imagining this man at all inclined to introspection. As he looked at the eager-faced Adelard, he wondered if the lad took after his mother. "How did he prepare you for the calling he longed for you to have?"

"He wanted me to hate the world and to see it as the cesspool of wickedness."

"And he taught you this by…"

"By encouraging me to watch others sinning when they did not know I was observing them."

Thomas bit his lip. He, too, had spied on others as a child to gain his father's favor. Was he so different from this lad? As he looked at this callow youth, lying in pain, he knew there was a dissimilarity between them. There was unhappiness but little torment in Adelard's eyes. Thomas had suffered the latter. Nonetheless, the young man required kindness.

"And how did you do this?" Perhaps the question might lead back to the issue of murder, while also allowing the young man to unburden himself of what weighed on him.

"At night, I followed men who lay with women not their wives." Adelard looked sheepish. "And put my ear to the wall as they committed adultery. Later, my father would ask for details of the sins I had discovered."

"Did he confront them with their sins?"

"Nay, Brother. He only wished to teach me the vile nature of men."

"Was lust the only sin he hated?"

"He condemns all seven of the deadly vices and blames our inability to reclaim Jerusalem from the infidels as proof of our laxity and wickedness. When the Jews came here, and Mistress Signy gave them shelter, my father railed at the impiety of doing so." Adelard frowned. "Then he grew even angrier when few would support him in condemning her."

"Many have been the recipients of her charity," the monk replied. Although she never shone a light on her virtue, few doubted the origin of the gifts placed at their doors when illness or death struck. "Continue."

"My father then asked me to spy on the Jews, certain that I would discover heinous things," the young man said. "If he could convey their wickedness to the village, he believed he could convince others that Mistress Signy was wrong in giving them shelter and that the Jews should be chased away from Tyndal."

Thomas felt his face flush with anger and forced himself into silence lest he utter curses against Adelard's father. However satisfying that might be, he knew that would only make the son defend Oseberne. Then an odd thought struck him, one that cooled his temper and pricked at him to question further.

"You say that your father hated all the deadly sins," the monk said, his tone calmer than he believed possible. "The Jews have long been reviled as money-lenders, the practice of usury being forbidden to Christians. Did he consider the wealth they acquired as a form of thievery?"

Adelard cried out, his eyes narrowed as if he suffered great pain.

"Is it your wound? I shall call Sister Anne."

"It is my soul that cried out, Brother."

"Then ease it, my son, and speak the reason." His own heart was pounding. What was he about to learn?

Adelard turned to Thomas, his face pale. "God has revealed my wickedness to you. My father did find their prosperity intolerable. He said they had no right to steal from Christians and for that reason he swore to recover what he could."

"And did he?" Thomas could not believe what he was hearing.

"When the travelers came to the inn, he ordered me to find where they hid their treasures. From what I told him, he planned the thefts." Adelard stared at the monk as if Thomas' face glowed like that of Moses returning with the Ten Commandments. "When I said that some had no more possessions than a beggar, he spat in contempt and claimed Satan had blinded me. There was no crime in taking worldly goods from any Jew, he said, for they had all stolen to serve the Devil."

So this was how the baker had acquired his growing wealth. For once, Sister Ruth had been right to question the providence of the golden candlestick for the altar at Tyndal. Prior Andrew had told him of the proposed gift and said he did not doubt that the gift was godly, even though the sub-prioress had. At the time, Thomas chose to ignore the nun's suspicions as well. Now he was ashamed and wondered who the true owner of that proposed gift had been.

As he listened to Adelard describe how his father had stolen the items, Thomas was surprised that Oseberne had been more clever than most. Many would have flaunted their new affluence, but Oseberne had revealed his increased wealth slowly, improving his ovens to produce better bread and suggesting that the finer product had greater appeal to merchants who came to market days from outside the village.

"How did your father sell the purloined objects?" the monk asked, when Adelard stopped to take breath.

"Some he sold to passing merchants in return for coin or plate. Others he had melted down." Adelard correctly read the expression on the monk's face. "No one from the village did this. He found a man willing to ask no questions as long as he received extra for his silence. After the Jews no longer traveled these roads, I did not see the man again."

Then nothing could be returned to the rightful owners, with the possible exception of one gold candlestick. Thomas uttered an oath under his breath. "And you hoped that your father's deeds might remain hidden from the crowner?"

Adelard nodded, his face gray with suffering.

"I fear that is not possible, my son."

But as much as Thomas longed to pursue this, he knew he must call Sister Anne to tend the youth now while he took this new information to his prioress. "You sinned," he said, "but it was done at the request of your father. Surely you see the evil of your deeds, but God is pleased when a heart repents. Be comforted. When you confess to me, your soul will be cleansed, although you may find the penance hard."

The youth's eyelids fluttered shut.

"For the present, you must sleep," the monk whispered. "Sister Anne will come to change your dressing. I shall return later. We can talk further then."

Adelard mumbled a reply but fell asleep.

As Thomas looked at him, he knew he must still resolve the question of why the silver cross had been found near Brother Gwydo's body. Turning to leave, he wondered how different this youth was from the hate-filled man who had fathered him. Maybe Adelard had killed Brother Gwydo, but he truly doubted it. Whatever the youth's faults, and he owned virtue enough, Thomas also felt some hope that he might choose a kinder life than Oseberne had.

"Sometimes," he murmured as he walked down the path to seek Prioress Eleanor, "I would like to believe that Man can be good."

Chapter Twenty-seven

Eleanor listened as both Ralf and Thomas conveyed what they had learned. She sat quite still in her audience chair, but her gray eyes shifted restlessly between the two men.

The monk turned to Ralf. "Do you see any cause to doubt Master Jacob's tale about Brother Gwydo? The story of their boyhood friendship could be confirmed, were you to question their old companions in Cambridge."

"I think he was telling the truth," Ralf said. "The man seems honest. After I left the house, I met Tostig on the way. He told me that he believed his prisoner to be a good man and that Master Jacob feared more for his family's safety than his own. In my experience, a guilty man worries most about his own neck."

"Or he may have decided he will hang simply because he is a Jew." Thomas knew he had spoken with a sharper tone than intended. "Knowing there is no hope for himself, the man may well fear for those he loves." Nor were these words any softer.

"Surely you do not think I would hang a man for murder just because he was not a good Christian?" The crowner's tone was curt. "If so, most men would find ropes around their necks, and I might be nervous of my own."

"I did not mean to offend. You have never sought the easy road to justice, Crowner, but others have," the monk replied. "From what little I have seen of Master Jacob, I am inclined to agree with you and Tostig. Whatever his faith, he speaks and behaves like any upright man."

Ralf looked ready to argue further, but Eleanor raised her hand. "We have no doubt of you, but your prisoner does not know your reputation for diligence in these matters. During the reign of King Richard, the sheriff of Yorkshire was complicit in the massacre of the Jews in York. That is but one example of the failure of the king's law, and our current king has recently demonstrated an inclination to retreat further from the protection traditionally promised his people. Do you not think the Jewish community has seen the same thing and grown fearful for their safety in this realm?"

Deflating, the crowner nodded.

"Therefore, let us turn our wits to better purpose and consider the new information and possibilities. You have both spoken of several. Shall we not set them against the facts and consider where that might take us?" There was a hint of impatience in Eleanor's voice. "Brother Gwydo was strangled and most certainly did not murder himself. His death after that of Kenelm suggests he was not the guard's slayer, but I think it likely he saw something he ought not to have witnessed."

"He might have aided another in Kenelm's death." Ralf looked uncomfortable.

"Even if he did, someone killed him as well. There is at least one killer who remains free, although reason suggests there is only one." Eleanor looked at both monk and crowner.

They nodded although Thomas' expression remained troubled.

"I also believe Mistress Gytha's tale." Eleanor's tone remained even, although she watched Ralf carefully. "She could not have slit Kenelm's throat, nor easily dragged him from the road to the priory millstream. Would you agree, Crowner?"

"She is a most honorable woman." He glanced away.

Eleanor raised an eyebrow but continued. "According to her, our lay brother found her unconscious in the forest and, when sense returned, he took her back to the priory grounds. She did not see Kenelm lying in the road where she left him. This suggests that the guard had already been taken to the mill pond.

Although we might argue that our lay brother committed the crime before he found Gytha, I find other details strongly rebut that conclusion." She waited for a moment.

Neither man had any comment.

"Master Jacob," she said, "has confided that his boyhood friend was horrified at the extent of violence perpetrated on the helpless in Outremer. For this reason, he felt remorse over his threats against his old friend after taking the cross, which is why he chanced my wrath and punishment to leave the priory and beg forgiveness for his words and actions."

"I can confirm that he hated violence, an opinion he expressed in our conversations before Kenelm's death and the arrival of this Jewish family. Such a man is unlikely to kill another for no reason," Thomas said.

"Might he have seen the attempted rape, become enraged, and sought to punish Kenelm?" Ralf opened his hand in a gesture that begged forbearance. "I ask only for the sake of discussion."

Thomas shook his head. "By dragging him into priory land, slitting his throat, and dropping him into the mill pond? Such violation of our land would be blasphemy for a man vowed to God's service. If he had responded out of anger as you suggest, would it not make more sense to drag the body into the forest?"

"You have argued well," Ralf replied.

"I confess that I cannot believe he would have killed a man at all, but, considering his fresh vows, I think he would have confessed it and thrown himself on the mercy of our prioress if he had." Thomas looked hopefully at her.

"I agree, Brother," Eleanor said. "When he begged to take vows, Prior Andrew and I examined him. Now I see we may have erred in failing to pose the questions we would have asked a man whose survival was not deemed a miracle, but he presented himself as humbled by the mercy God had shown in healing him. And, although he understood the war in Outremer was sanctioned by the Pope, he had seen too much bloodshed. We found his longing for a monk's life quite credible."

"I cannot argue with your reasons but that still leaves us with the question of why anyone would pollute God's earth with a murdered man's blood?" Ralf hit his palm with a fist in frustration. "I can think of no one."

"Of course, the Jewish family has been accused," Eleanor said, "condemned by a false legend in which they poison wells. Even if we were inclined to wonder if this one instance might be true, the facts disprove it. Not only why but how could one woman about to give birth, another with hands so twisted she could not assist in the birth, and a frightened husband slay the sole person who protected them from theft and other forms of persecution? So we must ask: who would profit by casting suspicion upon them, an accusation least likely to be questioned as evidenced by the village riot?"

"We have also not resolved the question of why the silver cross was found by Brother Gwydo's body. With great zeal, Adelard joined the rioters," Thomas said. "He might have killed Kenelm because the man protected the very people the youth believed were infidels. Since he thought our lay brother had sinned, he may have strangled him as well, and yet…"

"You believe him to have changed. When you spoke of Pope Gregory's letter, you said his certainty in the right to kill Jews was shaken." Ralf shrugged to suggest he found this explanation a thin one.

"He was attacked himself," Thomas added. "That is a stronger argument against his guilt."

"You are both reasonable men." Eleanor smiled, although the knuckles of her folded hands were white from gripping them together. "Might we conclude, for good cause, that Master Jacob is innocent of killing Kenelm and Brother Gwydo as well as the attack on Adelard?"

"To do any of those things would have put his family in danger, and he is not a fool," Ralf said.

Thomas nodded.

"Adelard may have had reason to kill Kenelm or even Brother Gwydo." The prioress looked at Brother Thomas.

"But he could not have attacked himself. I think he would have confessed murder to me, my lady. He is deeply troubled by fear of having offended God in light of what both Pope Gregory and St. Bernard have said. He also worries that his father has led him into sin by insisting he help with the thefts. Had he committed murder, his current state of mind would have driven him to cleanse his soul even at the cost of the hangman's noose."

"I do not share your belief that he would care more for his soul than his neck, but you have spoken to him. I have not." Ralf gnawed his finger.

"He has begged admission to the priory, Crowner," Eleanor said softly.

"You have never allowed a known murderer to take vows, my lady!"

"Nor would I now, but I mention it to suggest that some men do care more for their souls than their necks. Considering his prior interest in a monastic life, this one might."

He bowed with deference.

Eleanor acknowledged the gesture with grace but also knew that he had not changed his opinion. "Let me suggest another path to follow for a moment," she said. "Is Oseberne, the baker, our killer?"

"He stole from the Jews," Thomas said.

"So his son claims and further states that his father required him to spy on the travelers to determine what wealth they carried," the crowner replied. "Is the son's word trustworthy?"

"I believe it is," Thomas said. He had no proof, but Adelard could have accused his father of both stealing and murder earlier if he wanted to save himself. Instead, he had refused to talk to the crowner without first seeking a priest's advice. The youth's torment over his filial duty was convincing, and the only crime he said his father had committed was robbery.

"Is there a connection between the thefts and Kenelm's murder?" Eleanor gestured to the monk. "Can you see an argument in favor of that premise?"

"Kenelm was hired to protect the families after they suffered from thievery. He could have caught the baker stealing. Since the guard was reputed to love coin above honor, perhaps he demanded payment to remain silent." Thomas looked up at the ceiling.

Eleanor thought for a moment. "If he killed Kenelm, surely he was the one who pushed the body into our mill pond. He is a strong enough man to have done both. But why? He is a man of faith."

"To suggest that the Jewish family did it to poison our water, thus draping his crime in the robes of common myth. Kenelm was not liked here. Master Jacob and his family are hated for their faith. No one wanted a village man to be condemned." Thomas' face colored with anger. "Men are so easily turned away from displeasing truths by more satisfying lies."

"And Brother Gwydo might have been killed because he saw the baker kill the guard?" Ralf did not sound satisfied with the idea.

"If he had witnessed it, he would have come to me," Eleanor said. "He might have seen Oseberne do something that troubled him, but I doubt he saw him push the body into the pond. Again, he would have told me about that. I suspect he did not recognize the baker. Our lay brother knew few in the village." She turned to Thomas. "He took you to the place where the body entered the water but did not name any man."

The monk confirmed it. "Oseberne may have feared Brother Gwydo saw more than he actually did. Perhaps our brother heard a loud splash and only saw some man walk back to the road? He had no cause to question this further until he found the body floating in the pond. Then, as Brother Gwydo told me, he did examine the area further." Thomas clenched his fist. "In truth, there was no reason at all for the murderer to have killed our lay brother. Brother Gwydo saw nothing!"

"There is still the silver cross," Ralf said.

"What father casts blame on his son, knowing he might hang for a deed he did not commit?" Thomas' expression showed his outrage over such an act. "If the baker found the cross his son had lost, why would he drop it next to our lay brother's body? I may not like Oseberne's thievery, and may even believe him to be a killer, but I cannot accept that he would want his son to face a hangman's noose!"

"We do not know why the cross was dropped there," Eleanor said. "We could continue to speculate, but there is little value in that until we have more facts."

"I did find it some steps away," the monk said, unwilling to set this problem aside. "It is possible that the cross was never intended to cast guilt upon Adelard. Yet how can we accept that a father would strike his son so brutally and leave him for dead?"

"He might not have intended to kill his son," Eleanor said. "The attack took place near Master Jacob's stall." She turned to Ralf. "As you told me after you arrested him, if the village believed him guilty of killing Kenelm, a crime that took place some distance away, the villagers would be more likely to condemn him for a villainy committed just outside his door."

"Once again suspicion is cast upon the Jews," Ralf said, "as it was when the corpse was dropped into your pond."

"If the baker is guilty of Kenelm's death, he seems to have killed the one he thought might have witnessed the deed. We have no other reason for his assumed violence against our lay brother." Eleanor looked at each of the men, waiting for a response.

Thomas paled.

Ralf stared at the monk. "Which leaves one more in danger." He turned to the prioress, horror painting his face gray. "Where is Mistress Gytha?"

"Not within the safety of our priory," Eleanor said, color fleeing her cheeks as well. "Because we believed all danger was over, I gave her permission to visit her brother. She has left to..."

Ralf roared a curse that might have offended had it not been born of terror.

Eleanor leapt to her feet.

The heavy door of the chambers crashed against the wall.

The crowner had fled the room.

Chapter Twenty-eight

Nute had directed Gytha to the cooking shed behind the inn. As she turned the corner, she saw Signy in conversation with the inn's cook, a woman of impressive heft, a ruddy face, and autumn brown eyes. Her plump arms waved in the air like a fat bird attempting flight.

The innkeeper tossed her head back and laughed.

Although she had long known Signy, Gytha often marveled at the woman's beauty, a reaction shared by men and women alike. The red highlights of the innkeeper's blonde hair flashed in the sun. Her breasts promised intense joy, then soft ease to a fortunate lover. Yet this woman kept men at arms' length, dressed plainly, and devoted all her love to two adopted orphans and any villagers in need. The cook was one of the latter, a widow whose fisherman husband had drowned in a sudden gale.

Signy turned to see the prioress' maid and bid her join them. After sharing jests over one well known village sot, the cook pointed to the bubbling pot and asked for a critical tasting of her rabbit stew. Although Gytha never thought the cook had cause for worry, her skills adding to the reasons this inn was a favored stop on the road to Norwich, the maid dutifully sipped the broth and considered the flavor for a convincing moment. "The seasoning is perfect," she said with a broad smile.

The cook put a hand to her heart, looked to scudding clouds overhead, and exhaled with relief as if granted a miracle.

"Come," Signy said, taking Gytha's arm. As they walked away, the innkeeper bent toward the maid's ear: "You are troubled," she murmured.

"I need your advice."

"Stop for awhile, and you shall have my opinion, plain as it always is. Are you hungry or thirsty?"

Gytha shook her head.

"Not thirsty in this heat? Then your problem is no small thing. We shall talk in my room."

As they approached the small hut, a large dog rose to his feet and wagged his dusty tail. Signy greeted the happy beast with a soft touch, then gave him an even more welcome gift from the cooking shed. With a grunt of joy, he settled in to enjoy the meal.

The innkeeper invited Gytha to enter and shut the huge wooden slab of a door behind them. After she inherited the inn, she had replaced the small space allotted her as the inn's serving wench. Her uncle might have found an enclosed portion of the loft suitable for his needs, but his niece required a strong door and thick walls.

She pulled a bench away from the wall and offered Gytha a seat. The room was small but adequate for a woman with two small children. Against one wall, a few toys were neatly placed out of the way, as were the rolled-up bedding and straw-stuffed mattresses on which the children slept.

"It is Ralf," Gytha said with her accustomed directness.

Signy smiled. "Is he still unable to admit his love for you?"

The young woman blushed. "He has decided I am not suitable for him."

Looking down her nose, the innkeeper scoffed. "Now what has that foolish man done?"

Gytha hesitated, and then told the innkeeper about the struggle with Kenelm and her escape into the forest.

Taking her friend's hand, Signy expressed sympathy. "And you kept this to yourself? Not even telling your prioress? How you have suffered!"

"I was ashamed but would have confided in Prioress Eleanor had Kenelm not been murdered. Then I grew fearful, but she saw my turmoil and drew the truth from me. Because the man was killed, she said I must tell Ralf. Without doubt she was right, but the conversation with him turned cruel." Gytha spoke of his angry manner and rude questions. "Prioress Eleanor berated him for insulting my virtue," she said. "He sputtered and fussed, but she silenced him."

"Our prioress may be convent-raised, but she is no innocent," Signy said. "And the crowner will suffer from the wounds her sharp rebukes gave him." Nodding, she added, "Each pain is one he well deserves for his cruelty to you."

"Then I should not forgive him and am a fool to love him." Gytha looked away.

"All lovers are fools. It is our mortal nature, but that is no reason to turn your heart into stone." She reached out with gentle hand and made Gytha face her, noting her damp cheeks.

"But I must now seek another as husband."

"I did not say that. Ralf is a Norman and is no different from his ancestors who conquered our land under William the Bastard. He is rough, crude, and takes when he ought to beg leave."

That produced a brief smile from the prioress' maid.

"But his heart is tender, and he suffers when he hurts those he does not mean to harm."

Gytha sighed and waited for her friend to continue. She had never asked Signy if the crowner had once been her lover and had treated her ill, as rumors suggested. Nor would she mention it, for she felt no jealousy and loved Signy like a sister. What may have happened was long ago and long over. Like most women, Gytha believed that all Eve's daughters had the right to keep secrets in a world where truth often hurt women deeply.

"He loves you, lass, as does his daughter. He would marry you for Sibley's sake, if not his own, but it is the love he bears you that makes him draw back from confessing it. As he should, Ralf thinks he is too rough a man for the tender creature he sees in you."

"I am not bruised so easily," Gytha protested.

"Few of us are, but, when he looks at you, he sees skin as pink and soft as a rose petal in early morning. He studies his callused hands and worries they will mark you. He longs to wake up with your hair soft against his cheek, then rubs his prickly beard and fears it will scratch if he kisses you."

The innkeeper patted the young woman's hand, then stood, fetched a jug of cooled ale with two cups, and set them on the bench between them. She poured and passed a mazer to the maid. "And he should have qualms about marrying you, Gytha, for he will hurt you in many ways, some of which he cannot help."

"If you mean childbirth, I do not fear it."

"That was not all I meant. He is crowner here, a position that is honorable and appropriate to his birth but dangerous because of the crimes he must solve."

"It would be less perilous were he dishonest and accepted bribes, but I love him almost as much for his integrity as I do for his broad shoulders." Gytha blushed with a self-conscious smile.

"And aren't they though!" Signy laughed, then turned solemn. "That pursuit of true justice may bring him more trouble. King Edward rightly abhors the laxity allowed by his father in matters of law, but he may require an obedience that does not suit our crowner. Ralf has always kept to his own path. When his father died, he turned over his small inheritance to his eldest brother and became a mercenary, choosing to earn his own wealth. He came back a man of some means, more than any here would know from his stained clothes and scuffed boots, and is just as stubborn as he was before he exiled himself."

"Tostig says the brothers have made peace, and Sir Fulke frequents the king's court. Surely that provides Ralf some protection."

"Do not assume Sir Fulke would shield our Ralf. He was one of the few sheriffs to keep his post after King Edward returned to England and may believe that the king has granted him all the favor he dare expect. As for Ralf, we both know he is not a man who speaks softly or practices a graceful bow. He has refused to return to court or to marry another lady of rank. Instead, he remains here, chooses his friends amongst us and most probably his wife as well."

"That I shall not be. My brother may be honored with his friendship. He scorns me."

"Without doubt he has insulted you, but it was done in private. Most men would have shouted to all and sundry on market days that you were a whore, then called themselves virtuous for doing so. He did not do that."

"He has never treated me dishonorably until now."

"Although you are both virtuous and of worthy ancestry, Ralf stands higher in rank. Another man of his birth would have tried to make you his leman with no promise of wedding vows even if you quickened with his child."

Gytha flushed. "He has never begged me to share his bed, let alone lain with me against my will."

"Like most of his sex, Ralf wants to take a wife who is a virgin."

"As I remain."

Signy bent closer. "Of that I have no doubt, nor does your prioress, but consider what Ralf thought when he heard your story. He has behaved honorably, although I am sure it was with difficulty. Then he learned that another man tried to couple with you even if that was against your will. He was unable to think beyond the possibility that Kenelm might have stolen what he had wanted but denied himself. His rage blinded him to both truth and reason."

"Prioress Eleanor reminded him that virginity can be proven. He chose not to accept that or take my word. I find that intolerable."

Signy sipped her ale. "Ralf sinned against you. The difference between him and many others is that he regrets it and does not know how to beg forgiveness. For all his flaws, and he suffers many, he wants to be a good man and longs for a wife who knows him well, will listen to his doubts, forgive his weaknesses, but will keep all his secrets safe within her heart. That woman is you."

"You think he will ever ask my pardon?"

Signy's expression grew vague for a brief moment as if a forgotten memory had returned. She shook it away and smiled at the younger woman. "It will take him a while but he will. If he does, I advise you to forgive him. There are many men with greater wealth and softer hands that would wed you, but few of them are Ralf's match in other ways."

"I shall think on it as I go back to Tyndal," Gytha said. "You are a wise and good friend."

"Neither sage nor worthy, I am afraid, but merely selfish," Signy replied with a laugh. "If you married some fine merchant from the north or the south, I would lose your companionship."

Gytha bent over to kiss the innkeeper's cheek. The two women rose, and Signy accompanied her to the door. Outside, the dog panted in contentment after his fine meal. He wagged briefly when Gytha spoke to him as she passed by.

◇◇◇

Walking slowly back to the priory, she pondered what the innkeeper had said. Signy was wise, and she ought to take her advice. Although Gytha believed in charity, she never thought it prudent when reason suggested caution, but Ralf would not ridicule, beat her, or be disloyal. Indeed, he seemed to enjoy her teasing ways and blunt speech. Their times together had been warmed by good humor and easy conversation. He often sought her opinion and listened without disparagement. A goldsmith might drape her in rich ornaments. Ralf would give her gifts she valued more, even if he did lack in certain courtesies.

Near the mill pond gate, she stopped, remembering she had forgotten to visit Tostig as she had told the prioress she intended to do. At least he had not expected her, and he did have the prisoner to watch over. Perhaps it was best that she wait to visit him until after these murders were solved.

"Mistress Gytha! I am delighted to meet with you."

The voice was familiar, and the maid turned to reply with the grace expected.

It was a courtesy she regretted.

Chapter Twenty-nine

Ralf was drenched in sweat. Raising his fist, he beat against Oseberne's door with a ferocity that caused a dog trotting down the street to turn and flee.

No one answered.

He pounded again and shouted, threatening a myriad of plagues if no one answered his demand for entry.

Slowly the door inched open.

Ralf grasped his sword hilt.

A boy's spotty face appeared in the small opening, his eyes round with dread. "My lord?" His voice cracked between the two words.

Whatever ire he felt for the baker because of the crimes he believed he had and might still commit, the crowner did not wish to scare an innocent. Ralf swallowed his fury and tried to grin warmly. "Is your father within?"

The lad stared in silent terror at him.

Deciding that the sight of his teeth had probably reminded the baker's youngest of a hungry dragon, Ralf shut his mouth. "Your father? Is he home?" he asked with lips barely open.

The boy shook his head.

"Do you know where I might find him?"

Another head shake.

He hesitated. Presumably the boy was telling the truth. It usually took a few more years than this child owned to learn successful dissembling. "Ah, well," he sighed. "My need for his bread must wait."

"Shall I tell him that you would like to see him, my lord? Perhaps you could tell me what you require. I will let him know when he returns."

Ralf felt a sharp stab of guilt. "Nay, lad. It is of no moment. I am sorry I was so rude before. My intent was…" He had a hard time coming up with something that was far from his true purpose. How could he explain to this child that he wanted to find the father whom he might hang for murder? It was better not to finish the phrase. "Anon," he said, stepping back and waving.

The door was swiftly shut.

Grunting, the crowner turned in the direction of Tostig's house. As he kicked up dust marching down the road, he tried to convince himself that Gytha would be with her brother, as she told Prioress Eleanor she would. If so, he could almost hear Tostig roar at him for the insults he had dared to throw at his cherished sister: "Not virtuous? You are an ass, Ralf, one not even worthy of being one of my breeding stock!"

He groaned. Were Gytha safe and Tostig eager to pound him into the earth, Ralf would weep with joy.

Suddenly he was at his friend's door.

It was wide open.

He walked in.

Tostig and Jacob were sitting at the bench. Jacob was gesturing with enthusiasm as he explained the details of something involving wool. Gytha's brother frowned with interest and concentration.

Gytha was nowhere to be seen.

Tostig turned to see who had entered "Ralf! Welcome!" He gestured at a spot on the bench. "Share some ale with us. Master Jacob has been…"

"Where is your sister?"

Tostig stopped as he reached for the jug. Seeing the crowner's grim expression, he frowned. "I do not know. Why do you ask?"

"She told Prioress Eleanor that she was coming to see you."

"She has not been here."

Reading the meaning in the crowner's worried expression more quickly than Tostig, Jacob paled. "Has any harm come to her?"

"Where have you been this day?" Ralf knew the probable reply but was obliged to ask Jacob the question.

Tostig stiffened. "He has been with me."

"Nor has he ever let me out of his sight," Jacob said, his voice soft.

"I do not understand your queries, Ralf. Is my sister in danger or do you question my diligence?"

The crowner noticed that Tostig's hands had folded into fists. "Nay! The prioress had a task for her. I said I would carry the message, since I was on my way home. As for your prisoner, I had no doubt that he was here, but someone claimed to have seen him on the road. I swore to prove him wrong." Even though Ralf was not much given to prayer, this was one time he did ask God to let his friend believe this feeble tale.

Tostig was rarely shaken, but he not only bore his sister all the devotion a brother owed but he had been a father to her after their parents' deaths. Ralf was having problems enough keeping himself composed. He did not need to calm this man as well. Although he might often welcome assistance in his searches, he did not want Tostig, of all people, to join him.

Tostig's expression suggested uncertainty as to whether to believe his old friend or not, then he shrugged. "She might have stopped to visit with Mistress Signy before she came here."

Ralf glanced heavenward with gratitude. "Of course! She would want to see the innkeeper. I should have thought to stop at the inn first." He grinned and turned away.

"If you do not find her, Ralf, I assume you will let me know." Tostig's voice had acquired a sharp edge.

The crowner froze in the doorway. Not daring to face his friend, he simply nodded once and left. He did not trust himself to speak, fearing a greater betrayal of his growing terror.

◇◇◇

"She was here." Signy, unlike the brother, did not accept Ralf's swiftly crafted story. Putting her hands on her hips, she looked into his eyes and said, "I see that she is in danger. Even the unlettered could read that in your shifting gaze."

"Did she talk about Kenelm's murder?" He rubbed his hand across his eyes to dull the sting from his sweat as well as her look.

"We talked only about your boorish manner, but I doubt you came to hear about that. What do you want to know? Be direct, Ralf. It will save time."

"Nothing about who might have done the killing?"

"Nay." She tilted her head and waited.

"Where did she go after you had talked?"

"Back to the priory and not very long ago. You might have just missed her on the road."

"Not to her brother?"

"I stood in the door and watched her walk in the direction of Tyndal." She pointed. "Her brother's house is in the opposite direction, as you know well enough."

He groaned, spun around, and rushed out of the inn. As he ran down the road, he heard Signy shout something after him, but he did not hear what she said. Indeed, he did not care. If God was generous, He might grant him a second wish today, but the crowner knew better than to expect it.

◇◇◇

As he came to the bend in the road near the hut of Ivetta the Whore, he stopped to catch his breath. His heart pounded but not from running. There was no sign of Gytha. He began to tremble as fear grew like a foul growth.

What should he do? Surely he would have met her on the road by now. If he went all the way back to seek her in Prioress Eleanor's chambers, he would lose time if she had been captured but was still alive. If she were dead…

He cursed God, then insulted the Devil. It didn't matter which he offended if Gytha had been killed. God might send his blasphemous soul to Hell, but Satan could never torture him more than he would himself until the final Day of Judgement.

Ralf walked to the hut and paced back and forth, then stopped to listen as if hoping to hear her calling to him. Staring into the forest, he made his decision. Brother Gwydo's corpse was found there. There were places for a man to hide. He might still find Gytha alive, but in what state was a thought he did not wish to pursue.

Plunging into the woods, he took the shortcut some traveled to reach the hospital which lay closer to the priory's front gate than the one near the mill. But now he lost all control over his reason, and he rushed along like a madman, tripping on a root he did not see and then tumbling into a bush when he did not notice the rocks in the path. His foot twisted and he yelped like a pup. For a moment he lay where he had fallen and wept, not with the slight pain but from grief and anger.

Dragging himself out of the prickly branches, he twisted around to feel his tender ankle and asked why God would allow some monster to kill a virtuous, good-hearted and beautiful woman like Gytha, one who deserved only blessings for her kindness. It was a question to which he found no answer as he reached out to a branch and began pulling himself upright.

Something behind him snapped.

The blow that struck the back of his head threw him into a night no darker than the one in which his soul had already plunged.

Chapter Thirty

Thomas closed the mill gate and looked east toward the village, then back down the road to the west.

The crowner had disappeared.

Considering what he should do, the monk decided that Ralf must have gone to Tostig's house in case Gytha was there. Perhaps he would even stop at Oseberne's bakery to see if he could catch the man burning bloody clothes in his oven. To duplicate all that seemed a waste of time. If the crowner had found Gytha, he would soon be bringing her back to the priory. If he found Oseberne, he would take the baker into custody and question him. So where should he begin? Where might the crowner not yet have looked? With luck, he would meet Ralf somewhere.

At least Prioress Eleanor had sent him to offer what help he could. If she had not, he would have begged her to allow it. Until Gytha was found, he could not remain at peace. When his fellow religious went to chapel for the next Office, his spirit would have remained tethered to this earthly worry. He knew he should at least pretend to find complete comfort in prayer, but God would know him for a liar if he feigned to be better than he was.

He shuddered. There was another reason to join in the search for Gytha. Were the maid found dead, Thomas could at least offer her hovering soul the comfort of forgiveness. The prioress may have concluded the same when she sent him off.

"Please be merciful to those of us who love her," he murmured, "and to Mistress Gytha for her own sake."

Suddenly the monk heard something and looked down the road in the direction of the village.

A man was singing.

From around the bend, a chapman approached, his light stride suggesting that his pack of supplies was diminished and his travels were profitable. When he saw the monk, he raised his arm in greeting and evident pleasure.

"A blessing for a poor man who does not own a roof to keep the sun and rain from his head?" He rubbed the sunburned pate and grinned. "And perhaps a prayer to bring back the hair that once protected me from the weather?"

"I know of no remedy for the latter," Thomas replied with a laugh and gave the man's soul the ease he had begged.

The peddler dug in his pouch for a coin.

"The answer to an urgent question would be payment enough," Thomas said.

Looking surprised, the man replied: "If my poor wits are able."

"Did you see a tall man in the village, a man who wore a sword?"

"Aye. He was in a great rush to flee the place and preceded me here." He frowned, as if trying to remember something. "Near a clearing, he left the road."

"Was there a hut close by where he turned away?"

"Now that you have mentioned it, I did notice the place. Seemed odd that a man with a sword was walking into the forest. Common sorts don't own swords, and honest knights have horses." He looked over his shoulder toward the village. "Not an outlaw, is he?"

"He's our crowner."

"After a felon?" He still looked uneasy. "I hid for some time until I was sure he'd not return. My rounded pouch might tempt some."

"Looking for his wife, I think. She wasn't with him by any chance?" Thomas folded his hands and tried to look as if there was a marital issue here of which he did not quite approve. As for calling Gytha a wife, the title was only a matter of time in coming and thus no true lie.

The chapman grinned with relief. "Nay, he was alone. I hope he wasn't looking for a man who had put horns above his ears!"

Thomas shook his head and pointed to the leather bag at the peddler's waist. "I'd starve that pouch," he said, "if you wish to journey without fear of theft. As for the crowner and his wife, I shall find them and bring their discord to an end. You have given me the help I need to find them." Smiling, he bade the man farewell and walked off. At least he knew that Ralf was still hunting for the maid. He would look for him in the forest.

Glancing back, Thomas watched the chapman hide coins, until his pouch had grown thin, and then disappear over a small rise on the road running alongside the priory wall. Quickly, the monk slipped into the brush, seeking the footpath that led to the village. It was a route he knew well since he had lived in that small hut, named for a poor woman now dead, when he chose to live in contemplative solitude away from the community of Tyndal Priory.

The sunlight faded as he went deeper into the thick brushwood and trees. Dry leaves had already begun to drop on the earth long softened by their decay. Thomas walked carefully and listened for voices above the humming of insects and the whistling of a soft sea breeze that moved through the branches above him.

Then he stopped and held his breath.

He had heard a laugh.

Slipping to the ground, Thomas hoped he had not been seen. From just a short distance ahead of him, he was now certain he heard more voices.

One was a woman's.

Like a cat stalking a bird, he slid on his belly and inched toward a large rock near a tree, both of which provided good cover. From between the two, he could safely look into a small clearing.

Gytha and Ralf were sitting on the ground. Both were bound.

Oseberne stood over them, a glittering knife in his hand. "I would not mock, if I were you," he said to Gytha. "I am master here." He glanced down at Ralf and nudged the crowner with his boot. "A traitorous sort you are, protecting infidels when you should have used the flat of your sword to send them on their way."

"They are under King Edward's protection." Ralf shifted away from the baker's foot.

"The king has no love for Jews," Oseberne snapped. "He fought unbelievers in Outremer. Do you think he does not know how they defile the very earth they touch?"

"Say what you will, but the Jewish family here did not cut Kenelm's throat and dump his body into the mill pond, befouling priory water."

"They might have done!"

"You did it and cast blame on innocents."

"No unbeliever is innocent. Saying otherwise tells me that you have taken the Devil's hand, Crowner."

"Why kill Kenelm?"

Oseberne crouched and flicked his knife back and forth in front of Ralf's face. "He caught me stealing from the Jews when the innkeeper gave them shelter last winter. Thereafter, I paid him a reasonable fee to turn his back on occasion when I took from those people what they had stolen from Christian men. He got greedy when this new family came and demanded more, threatening to tell you." He pointed the knife at Ralf. "I saw no need to suffer the penalty of an unjust law when all I did was recover illegally obtained goods."

"You were only enriching yourself." Gytha pushed herself up against a tree trunk.

The baker pointed his blade tip at her. "I would not cast such an accusation at a respected man, whore. You struck Kenelm first, a blow he did not deserve after you had driven the man into unlawful lust. Was he unwilling to pay your usual fee?"

"He followed me. I did nothing to encourage him." Her face turned scarlet with fury.

He licked his lips. "I've watched you flaunt yourself on market days. Had I been as weak-willed as Kenelm, I might have lain with you myself, but God has kept me chaste since my wife's death."

"With impotence, most likely," Ralf growled.

Oseberne leapt to his feet, his face turning purple. "Do you long to become a gelding, Crowner?"

In his hiding place, Thomas winced. He had no doubt that the baker would kill Gytha and Ralf. How Oseberne planned to stage this crime did not take much imagination. All he need do was spread the rumor that Gytha had whored with Kenelm and that Ralf had slain her out of jealousy, then killed himself in shame and grief. There were few in the village who did not know that the crowner hoped to make this maid his wife.

Thomas knew he must do something, but Oseberne, who was his match in height and strength, had a knife. Glancing around, he found nothing to use in defense. He clenched a fist and wished it held a mace.

Ralf said something too soft to hear.

"Fool! Say rather that I was clever and took the chance to remove the midge that was bleeding me of coin and, at the same time, cast blame on a wicked people. After I saw this whore running into the woods, I heard Kenelm groan and helped him to rise. There was a bloody rock nearby. She must have stunned him with it, I thought, and suddenly I knew God had shown me favor! He had given me the perfect opportunity to render proper justice on those deserving punishment."

Rather it is Satan who sings sweetly into the ears of men who want God to justify the cruelties they wish to commit, Thomas muttered to himself.

"I told him I would get him to the hospital and so supported him into the priory grounds. There I slit his throat and threw him into the pond. Unfortunately, as I was leaving, I noticed the lay brother some distance behind me. Although I concealed myself in the shadows of the outside wall, I feared he had recognized me."

"So you killed Brother Gwydo? He was a good, kind man…" Gytha squirmed in outrage.

"Good? He fled the priory that same night! How can you praise one who claimed piety but surely left to commit hidden sins?" He snorted. "Did you lie with him too? My son thinks so."

"If gentleness has become a transgression, then Brother Gwydo excelled in wickedness," she hissed at him. "I know of no other evil he ever did."

"God did not agree. When the riot started, I feared my bakery might suffer harm, no matter how righteous the cause against the Jews. So I came to the priory to bring back this lackluster crowner." He kicked Ralf forcefully in his ribs. "I saw the Devil's creature slip once more into the woods, followed him, and sent him to Hell. If God had not wished the death, He would not have let me see the man again. Not only did I eliminate a witness to Kenelm's death, but I served God by punishing a sinful monk."

The crowner gritted his teeth, not wanting the baker to know how much pain he had caused. "And made sure your son was blamed for Brother Gwydo's murder. Brother Thomas found the silver cross near the corpse."

"I had picked up my son's cross where it had fallen on the ground near my house. Another proof that God favored my deed, for I had the cord ready to strangle the lay brother. I granted him a mercy, despite his sins, and briefly dangled the cross in front of his eyes so he might die in the knowledge of what he had betrayed."

Gytha sobbed.

Suddenly, the glow of certainty faded in Oseberne's eyes. "I did not realize I had dropped it and grieve that the accident has cast suspicion on Adelard." He frowned. "Yet he must deserve punishment, for he dared to question the truth I had so carefully taught him about hating sinners and unbelievers. This was wisdom taught to me by a holy man of God! Instead, my son chose to believe lies about a pope and a saint, told by a man who had so little faith he could not remain a hermit." He spat.

Thomas eased himself into a crouch. He had little time to stop the baker. He must use surprise as his shield and pray that God gave him the strength to overpower the man.

Oseberne smiled and looked carefully at one of his prisoners, then at the other. "Now I shall complete God's will and kill you both. Pity that there is no priest to hear your confessions, but no one who gives comfort to the Devil's people, as you both have done, deserves a chance to escape Hell." He raised his knife. "First, the whore!"

Ralf roared and, with amazing strength, threw himself head-first at the baker's legs.

Oseberne laughed, easily stepped aside, and drove his knife into the crowner's back.

Then he turned to the wide-eyed Gytha.

Chapter Thirty-one

Thomas leapt over the rock and charged into the clearing. Roaring with the fury of an enraged demon, he lunged at Oseberne.

The baker stumbled back. Seeing the monk in a shaft of sunlight, his red hair glittering like fire, Oseberne screamed, dropped his knife, and fled. He crashed into the woods, shrieking like a terrified beast.

Thomas tried to follow, but he slipped in the decaying leaves and fell. By the time he had scrambled back to his feet, the baker had disappeared. Then he looked at his bleeding friend and knew he must let the killer go.

Thomas knelt by the crowner's side.

"Catch that Satan's spawn," Ralf hissed through clenched teeth.

Suddenly the hair on the back of his neck rose, and Thomas knew that someone was standing behind him. He grabbed the fallen knife, jumped upright, and spun around.

It was Gytha. "Cut this last knot, Brother. I'll stay. The baker must not escape." She showed him her loosened bindings.

"He was no sailor to tie this poorly," Thomas said as he swiftly freed her.

"I was not fast enough but had worked them loose against the tree trunk." Gytha fell to her knees beside the crowner. "Leave this rooster to me," she said, pressing a handful of her robe against his wound. "Our crowner is too tough to die just yet." The tone may have been abrupt, but the tears on her cheeks spoke of caring.

Ralf groaned.

"Go quickly," Gytha begged as she began ripping strips of cloth from her chemise.

For an instant, Thomas hesitated, then ran toward the woods where the baker had fled. With luck, he might find men to help him catch the killer. Oseberne was too strong to subdue without assistance. After his experience at Baron Herbert's castle, the monk was loath to use violence, but, if God was willing to grant only one favor, Thomas would choose the capture of this killer.

Shoving aside branches and jumping over shrubs and scurrying creatures, the monk raced through the forest. When he finally emerged onto the road, he looked toward the village.

The baker stood panting at the mill gate.

"Stop!" Thomas knew his command would be ignored but hoped that someone nearby would hear his cry.

Oseberne pulled open the gate, slipped inside, and slammed it shut.

Had the baker locked it? Thomas kicked the gate. It flew open, and he ran through. Why was the baker trying to escape through priory grounds?

The baker fled down the path by the mill pond, shoving aside a young woman who had her child by the hand.

Thomas paused by the fallen mother and stretched forth his hand.

The woman waved him on.

Now he had to run faster to catch up. "Surrender!" he shouted again, but the effort took too much breath.

This time, Oseberne turned his head. He pointed in the direction of the church. "Sanctuary!" he screamed. "I shall throw my arms around the altar. You cannot have me arrested! God sees fit to protect me."

"You'll hang for murder," Thomas roared and found strength to gain speed. "Never will I let you escape punishment for killing gentle Brother Gwydo, casting blame on innocent people, and trying to send your own son to the hangman," he gasped. Suddenly, his feet felt so light he doubted they touched the ground. Had God given him wings?

Abruptly, the baker veered off the path and fled down into the grove of fruit trees.

It took Thomas a moment to understand that the man was taking a shortcut to the church, thus avoiding anyone else on the path who might slow or stop him. The monk slid down a low rise from the road to follow and was outraged when he saw the baker running into the place where Brother Gwydo had set up his bee skeps.

The change in direction cost him momentum, and Thomas found it harder to catch his breath. Gritting his teeth, he willed himself to continue. The baker must not reach the safety of the church.

Oseberne looked over his shoulder to see how close Thomas was. He shouted again.

Thomas neither understood nor cared what the baker had said. Entering the meadow, he cursed. Here the ground was rough, and he was forced to watch his footing.

He heard something and glanced up.

Oseberne had stumbled. Stretching out his arms to keep his balance, his hand struck a skep. The woven basket turned over and bumped another, causing both to topple to the ground.

The baker fell to his knees.

Thomas cried out in triumph.

Suddenly a cloud of bees erupted from the damaged skeps. The buzzing grew louder as they flew toward the baker.

Thomas froze.

Oseberne struggled to get to his feet. The swarm landed on his head and neck. His face turned dark with their churning black bodies. He screamed once, gasping for air, and clawed at his face and throat. Then he collapsed on the ground.

Some of the bees dropped beside their victim. Others flew away.

Oseberne did not move.

Thomas stood quite still. Fearing he would be attacked by the bees as well, he waited until the swarm dispersed. Then he moved slowly forward.

The baker lay where he had fallen.

The monk edged closer.

Oseberne's eyes bulged, staring as if he had just seen the maw of Hell. His swollen face was pocked with scarlet wounds from the bee stings, and his tongue protruded obscenely from his mouth.

Thomas had no doubt that the baker was dead when he knelt beside him. Out of duty, he uttered a perfunctory offer of forgiveness to the hovering soul for any sin truly repented, then he jumped to his feet.

As he ran to the hospital to bring help for Ralf, he acknowledged that he cared little about the baker's soul. God might choose to forgive Oseberne's sins. Thomas would not.

Chapter Thirty-two

Thunder rumbled in the distance. Black clouds from the sea covered the blue sky in mourning. The sun hid, and grey shadows slipped into the audience chamber, bringing their attendant gloom.

Adelard knelt before Prioress Eleanor and Prior Andrew. The youth's eyes were red from weeping, and his hands shook as he positioned them into a prayerful attitude.

Andrew looked down at the lad, his expression a blending of dismay and sorrow. "We shall pray for your father's soul, my son," he said and then stopped as if thinking how he might best continue. "If his heart regretted the sins he committed, God will judge his soul with greater mercy."

The young man shook his head. "Your kindness is beyond my ability to repay. For all of my life, I looked to my father for guidance and tried to honor him as we are told we must." He stopped, unable to find words that would express what he might, or ought, to feel.

"However, his sins belong to him alone," Prioress Eleanor said. "It is your duty to confront your own, as each of us must do." She nodded at her prior.

"Confess fully, follow the wise guidance offered, and beg for the strength to become a more compassionate and virtuous man." Andrew glanced back at his prioress with a doubtful look.

"I did help him in his thefts." Adelard spread his hands in a gesture of despair.

"At his command, an order you felt bound to obey. The crowner has agreed not to charge you as long as there is proper recompense for the crime." Eleanor emphasized the last phrase.

"What can I do about the stolen goods? I do not know the names of those from whom the items were stolen. Some have been melted down beyond recognition. Most have been turned into coin."

Eleanor indicated that he should rise. "All coin must be given to the poor and suffering. Mistress Signy knows best where help is needed. Take it to her, as much as you can garner, for almost all your father's wealth was gained from stealing."

"The golden candlestick?" He staggered to his feet and looked away, unwilling to look the prioress in the eye. "Shall it not be placed on the priory altar to honor God, as my father promised? It was to be my gift when I took vows here."

"We shall not accept it," she replied, her tone sharp. "It is tainted with blood and offered in sin. It, and the few remaining items, will be sent back to the Jewish community in Norwich. Master Tostig can sell the melted gold and return the profit there as well. In doing all this, you earn a pardon for the crime you committed at your father's behest."

"Then I have no hope of entering Tyndal as a novice!" His words ended with a cry of pain.

"Are you sure your vocation is your own and not a shadow of your father's old longing?" Prior Andrew leaned against the window and looked out across the priory lands toward the forest where Brother Gwydo had died.

"I have a true calling!"

Eleanor's smile lacked warmth. "That assertion we must carefully test with more rigor than we were obliged to apply before your father's death. Under the circumstances, we have no choice."

"I swear to do anything, my lady." Once again, he fell to his knees.

"You have much penance to fulfill for yourself."

"I have confessed fully to Brother Thomas. My errors may have been sins, but they share guilt with good intentions. He said that he would leave the method of expiation to you both."

"Should you agree with this proposal, I am sure that Brother Thomas would concur that these acts will cleanse your soul and prove whether you have a genuine vocation."

He nodded eagerly.

"Do you not have a brother who is still a child?"

As if he had forgotten all about him, Adelard looked confused, then confirmed that he did possess a younger sibling.

"Were you to enter the priory now, he would have no one to feed or cloth him."

"God takes care of sparrows," the youth suggested hopefully.

Andrew spun around and glared. "God did not suggest that we should willfully abandon the helpless. He may feed the birds of the air, but He does so by plan and not by turning His back on their needs."

Eleanor looked at her prior with amazement, unaccustomed to hear him speak so roughly.

Looking down, Adelard blushed but then mumbled: "He would be left to the kindness of villagers. Perhaps Mistress Signy…"

"Our good innkeeper has already taken two orphans," Eleanor said. "You have no right to demand she do more when you have done so little."

As if struck, he winced.

Eleanor told the prior to continue.

"Now hear what your penance should be, one that matches the sins you have committed in deed and in thought." Andrew watched the youth put his hands over his head as if fearing blows, but no pity showed on the prior's face. "You shall take over your father's business, make it profitable in an upright way, and train your younger brother to become a master baker. When he has proven his skill, and is old enough, he may take over the shop."

Adelard gasped. "He is a child! It'll be years before he can be ready. My father taught him almost nothing."

Andrew waved away the objections.

"If I must." The youth bowed his head once more.

"As you know, you have little earned from honest labor to give the priory should you beg admittance." Andrew shifted his weight to his good leg.

The young man slumped back on his heels. "Since you will accept nothing in any form that was taken from the Jews and insist I rebuild my father's business again solely to profit my brother, you have made it impossible for me to acquire the gift needed to enter here with honor."

"If you surrender all that was taken from the king's people to Mistress Signy and Master Tostig, become a good father to your little brother, and turn your steps onto the path of kindness, charity, and selflessness, we shall consider your penance done. Should your most ardent desire remain entrance to this priory, after your brother becomes skilled and of an age to take over the baking, you may approach us again."

He blinked. "I shall be an old man by then."

Andrew shrugged "That is of no moment. There are those who take on the full weight of austere vows when they are so ill and bent with pain that the burden of doing so is onerous indeed. You must have the opportunity to understand fully what you are giving up. By then, you should know whether you wish to leave a soft bed for a thin mattress, kneel on icy stones when the earth itself is frozen, exchange wine and meat for ale and fish, and own one rough habit in which to survive the chill of winter."

"Time and prayer shall inform you," Eleanor said and carefully watched the youth.

Adelard frowned. His silence suggested that the ardor of his claimed vocation might have subtly weakened.

Eleanor noticed this hesitation and quickly told him the final penitential requirement. "As Prior Andrew has said, we would then consider admitting you as a lay brother without asking a gift, for we must refuse anything that would impoverish your brother. He is innocent of all that has occurred."

"A lay brother labors in the fields! I know Latin. I should become a choir monk, a priest, a man who stands before God to sing the Offices…"

"The rank of a faithful soul is determined by purity of motive and sincerity of service." Eleanor's tone was icy.

"Do you accept this penance?" Andrew stood before the young man and cupped Adelard's chin, raising it so the youth was forced to look him in the eye.

"Do I have any choice?" Adelard grumbled and then raised his eyes upward. He began to tremble as if something were shaking him. "I accept," he whispered.

Eleanor's expression glowed with benevolence. "We shall look forward to soon hearing from Mistress Signy about your generosity to the poor."

"Go back to the world," Prior Andrew said, "confess often, and cast off the arrogance which led you to so many grievous sins."

Adelard rose to his feet, his face pale. He looked from one to the other as if begging for a softer penance. When neither prior nor prioress granted him that silent wish, he bowed and rushed away.

The young nun, who had been standing just inside the room, closed the door the youth had left open in his hurried flight.

Eleanor turned to her prior. "Shall we ever see him at our gate again, begging enclosure within our walls?"

"I think not." Andrew did not look disappointed. "But let us hope that he has learned from the sins he committed and becomes a virtuous man."

"Our sub-prioress must be thanked for her insights," Eleanor said with a fleeting smile. "It was she who doubted his suitability when you and I were otherwise inclined to accept his plea."

"That will give her much pleasure," Andrew replied, his mouth puckered as if he had just drunk wine turned sour.

With that, Eleanor laughed. It was a relief to find some merriment after all the sorrow of the last few days.

◇◇◇

Outside, the rain started to fall, the drops heavy and thick. As if cleansing the land, the wind drove the downpour like flung pebbles across the ground. By morning, the scoured earth would once again be sweet.

Chapter Thirty-three

Thomas stood at the edge of the meadow and looked at Brother Gwydo's bee skeps. The two damaged by Oseberne lay deserted on the ground. Perhaps those bees had found a liege lord in another skep, or so he hoped. That they might have suffered because a cruel man committed a thoughtless act was an idea he could not bear.

He shut his eyes, lifted his face to the sun, and listened to the sounds of living things. Were he inclined to idle dreams, he might have imagined that the world just heaved a sigh, grateful that the killing was over. He wondered if it also regretted the death of a kind man, one who had turned away from bloodshed and longed for a quiet life.

But did violence ever end, even on lands placed under God's rule? Tyndal Priory had suffered its own share of murders from the first day he had come here. In his darkest hours of melancholy, he feared he had brought the pale horseman with him like some plague. Yet Prioress Eleanor had arrived shortly before him, and all knew that unlawful Death was no boon companion of hers.

Opening his eyes to escape back into the sunlight, he rubbed the sleeve of his robe across his cheeks. They were damp with tears.

"You are sad, Brother."

Turning around, he saw Tostig just a few feet behind him.

"Only pensive," Thomas replied with a reassuring smile.

The man knelt and stretched his hands out to the monk. "You saved my beloved sister, Brother. I shall always remain in your debt for that gift."

"We must both thank God for guiding me there," Thomas replied and begged Tostig to stand. "I can claim no greater virtue than to have been His instrument in that moment."

"Then what offering may I give Him in thanks?" Tostig looked around as if the answer might appear before him. "However inadequate, something is required. A sister owns a place in any brother's heart, but Gytha has been like my own child."

Thomas did not know Tostig well, but he had heard that the Saxon was a man who rarely revealed his thoughts and never his emotions. Hearing the man's voice shake, the monk realized just how deep his devotion to his sister was. Perhaps he could offer a suggestion, one that might permit two people, for whom he cared as well, some happiness.

"You might forgive our crowner for speaking in a manner he profoundly regrets," Thomas said. From Prioress Eleanor he had learned that Gytha had not visited the crowner, as was her former wont, and that Tostig knew the reason for this change. "Had he not put his own life at risk, I would not have been quick enough to save your sister's."

Tostig did not smile, but there was a hint of amusement in his eyes. "To forgive or not remains my sister's choice. As for me, I have known the man too long. His heart and his mouth are often at odds, and the latter does not always express his better nature. I shall speak on his behalf to her, but doing so is a small thing and not worthy enough of my gratitude to God."

"Then I can only suggest that you consult our prioress."

"I am unable to match what the baker offered, and I know how deeply Sub-Prioress Ruth must regret the lost altar candlestick. Sadly, I own no gold."

"Oseberne's wealth was stolen. Prioress Eleanor has refused to accept anything he once touched. Whatever you offer is an honorable gift."

Tostig stiffened. "A Saxon is allowed to claim honor in a world ruled by Normans?" Then he flushed. "Forgive me, Brother. That is an ancestral wound which refuses to heal, but I should not have allowed its stench to pollute holy air. I did not mean to offend. As you surely know, I hold both you and your prioress in the greatest esteem."

"She knows that well, Tostig. As for me, I am told that my mother was not of Norman birth. If so, then only half of me might be offended, and that half swore to follow the teaching of one who forgave all, even the Romans who killed him. Shall I do less over a matter that is so trifling in comparison?"

"You are a good man, Brother Thomas." Then he looked away for a moment before facing the monk again with a puzzled expression. "I long for wisdom on another matter. May I ask your advice?"

Thomas nodded.

"Jacob ben Asser and I found we owned much common ground while he was imprisoned in my house. Is it odd, or even sinful, that one of his faith and one of mine could do so?"

Thomas turned thoughtful. "I found him to be a good man, one who, like you, has valid grievances in this world ruled by others of different heritage and, in his case, faith. Yet he loves his family and cheerfully greets those who approach him with good will, much as you do yourself." He stopped for a moment, faced with his own, sudden and turbulent, whirlpool of unformed questions. Pushing them aside, he gave Tostig the reply that would most ease the man's troubling doubts. "That you both felt kinship is not surprising, but I think God had a hand in this. While others of our faith threatened his family with cruel murder, you showed him the compassion that our Messiah taught us to practice. Your example may one day bring him to salvation."

"I shall find comfort in that, Brother." Tostig looked relieved. "He and I did speak of cooperating in a wool venture. If I can purchase the needed sheep and should he leave England, I will have an honest representative…"

Tostig continued, but Thomas drifted into his own perplexed musings. Ben Asser was a virtuous man, loving and caring to his wife and mother-in-law. He might have been angered by the insults and acts of Kenelm and Adelard, but he had truly turned the other cheek, despite all provocations. How was it possible that a Jew be more righteous than a Christian? The difference, of course, was in the acceptance of the Messiah, but scripture also made it clear that God had not abandoned those He had first chosen as His beloved people. Thomas was baffled.

Furtively, he glanced upward, directing the problem to God and was greeted with heavy silence. The monk sighed. His list of unanswered questions was growing longer, but God had never shown displeasure with the asking. On occasion, and in His own time, He had even replied.

Suddenly, Thomas was aware that his companion had stopped talking.

Gytha's brother was grinning at him.

"Forgive me," the monk said.

"I had just said that I know someone knowledgeable about bees, Brother. If I pay his wages, do you think your prioress will accept that from me as gratitude for my sister's life?"

Thomas almost said that his prioress was just as thankful that Gytha was not dead, but he knew the man needed to proffer this gift. So he swore to bring the proposal to Prioress Eleanor and said he thought she would be pleased.

Tostig brightened, thanked the monk, and left, walking through the meadow where the bees let him pass in peace amongst them.

"I have no reason to be here," Thomas murmured.

Turning from the place where Oseberne had died, Thomas walked back to the path that led from mill gate to the monks' quarters. Sorrow lashed at him. His friendship with Brother Gwydo had begun but a short time ago when he first heard the lay brother sing, but he had found a rare comfort in the man's company from the beginning. Not only would he miss one who was good even to God's small creatures, but he grieved that he could never know such a man better.

When tears once again stung his eyes, Thomas did not stop them from flowing down his cheeks.

Chapter Thirty-four

Ralf rubbed his bristled chin and glared at the table. Today's gifts included a jug of fresh ale from Tostig, a parsley-dotted mushroom pie with sweet onions from Sister Matilda, and a dish of berries plucked by his daughter. He did not disdain the bounty, but his spirit was too heavy to enjoy them. The berries he would force himself to eat. The rest he would give to others. Normally a man of hearty appetite, he had lost weight.

"My lord?"

"Yes," he snapped with sharp annoyance. He hated to be called that. As a third son he owned no title. His knighting on the battlefield years ago was an honor he kept so secret that even his eldest brother did not know of it. His reasons for doing so may have been founded in an old yet raw bitterness, but he was also a contrary man. The only title he allowed himself was that of crowner.

"You have a visitor from the priory." The voice was muffled.

The woman did not even stick her head around the corner. Did she fear he sat here stark naked? "Tell Brother Thomas that I am not able to enjoy his company," he growled and almost added that the woman was safe from him except, perhaps, on nights with a full moon when he might grow a tail and acquire hooves.

"Then I shall relay your message," a voice said, now quite clear.

As if lightning had just struck him, every muscle in his body turned numb.

Gytha walked through the door and put her basket down on the table. "I heard that you refused to let the lay brother shave you, and from the look of you, you haven't changed your clothes since Brother Thomas came upon us in the forest." She wrinkled her nose. "A bath would not be amiss. I understand that even our king does not find the practice offensive."

He grunted and would not meet her eyes.

"Sister Anne sent me with fresh bindings and newly picked herbs for your wound." She tilted her head to one side and studied him. "Or would you rather rot?"

"Rot."

"Sibely needs her father."

"I am here for her."

"The father she loves? Nay, rather a thing that looks like a wild boar and acts like a lumbering bear. You must frighten the child."

"I am unworthy of her love."

"And which man is not from time to time? But you are not without some merit. If I remember correctly, you would not be sitting there with that gash in your back if you hadn't tried to save my life."

He looked away and scratched at his beard.

"Very well, then, choke on your black bile. In the meantime, whether you want it or not, I have come to change your dressings. Sit on that bench. I refuse to stand on a stool to do this."

He obeyed, eased the clothes off his back, and muttered something that might have been a phrase of gratitude. Somewhere outside, he heard bright voices and recognized his child's laugh. Did he truly scare her?

"The wound is healing well," Gytha said, tossing the old binding aside and examining the deep cut. "No thanks to the care you have taken of it." She pushed him forward and poured wine into the injury without warning.

He yelped.

"Have you considered the possibility that God must have meant you to live for some purpose? Had the knife entered here rather than here, you would be dead." She reached over to get something out of the basket. Her arm brushed against his.

The soft touch was more than he could bear. Ralf bit his lip.

Gytha rebound the wound in silence.

Suddenly, a little girl flew through the door, ran up to Gytha, and threw her arms around the young woman's legs. "You have come back!" she squealed. "Da! Mistress Gytha is back! Tell her she must stay now. You missed her too. You said so."

Gytha reached down and lifted Sibely into her arms, covering the child with kisses. Then she put her down and the two of them danced in a circle, the little one giggling and Gytha singing a familiar song.

From the doorway, the child's nurse peeked around the corner, laughed in delight, and then quickly disappeared.

Stopping to catch a breath, Gytha bent down to place another kiss on the child's head. Sibley refused to release her hand and pointed with the other to the red berries still in the dish. "You haven't eaten them, Da. Did you not like them?" A worried frown creased her smooth brow.

Ralf could not bear to see the innocence of her face marred with any worry. "I was about to ask Mistress Gytha to bring them to me." He looked at the maid with a sheepish expression. "If she would, that is?"

Gently releasing her hand, Gytha smiled at Sibley and reached for the dish. "Your father has been resting, as he was told he must by Sister Anne. I am sure he just awoke and not seen your gift 'til now." She shot the crowner a playful look, then handed him the glistening plump fruit. "He shall love the taste. These are just what he should have to regain the strength needed to lift you to the heavens as he was wont to do. Did you and your nurse pick these?"

Sibley nodded vigorously and proceeded to tell Gytha just where and when the fruit had been found, then how it had been picked, berry by berry.

As he watched, Ralf wanted to both laugh and weep. These two were the ones he loved most on this earth. In truth, he would die before he let anyone hurt either, and yet he had caused great pain to the one who now knelt in front of his daughter and asked for even more details about all she had done to harvest the fruit.

Finally, Gytha stood, then bent again and kissed the little girl's cheek.

Sibely grabbed her hand. "Stay," she whispered. "I did not like it when you did not come every day." Then she turned to her father. "Please tell her not to leave again like she did?"

Ralf swallowed hard. "Go find your nurse," he said gently, "and I shall speak with Mistress Gytha in private."

As if summoned by some invisible messenger, the nurse slipped through the entrance, knelt, and held out her hands to the child.

Sibely hesitated, still looking at Gytha.

"I must speak with your father, but I shall come soon for a kiss."

Dutifully, but with evident reluctance, the child went to her nurse, and the pair disappeared. There were no sounds of laughter outside.

Ralf put the berries down and cleared his throat. "Whatever quarrel you have with me, will you not visit my child? She is an innocent in all that has happened between us and loves you dearly."

Gytha bowed her head. "You ask something that I would be most willing to do." Then she looked back at him with sadness. "But I must ask if you think it wise to expose her to one whom you find contemptible."

Ralf slammed his fist on the table, then cried out in pain.

Gytha reached out and grabbed his arm. "You will reopen the wound!"

Tears were rolling down his cheeks, and he stretched out his hand. "In answer to your question, I pose this one to you: why care whether I live or die, a man who insulted you with no cause and cast dishonor on you, a woman whom he holds in the greatest respect?"

She moved away from him. "It is my Christian duty to pardon those who injure me, but I would lie if I claimed to be strong enough in faith. I do not forgive easily."

"Shall you never pardon my transgressions against you?"

Gytha folded her arms and tilted her head as she gazed at him without speaking.

"I have long wished to plead for a far greater favor but dared not," he whispered. "Perhaps I never had a right to beg it of you, but now I have no hope."

"Voice it, my lord," she replied, her voice steady but soft. "I promise to listen, even if I cannot grant your request."

"Marry me," he murmured and bowed his head.

She cupped her reddening ear and bent forward. "Speak louder for I cannot understand you."

"I love you," he said, only slightly louder.

"I cannot have heard you correctly."

"Shall I kneel before you as I ought to one I worship?" Ralf reached out an imploring hand.

"Do not injure yourself by doing so. I am but a frail woman and unworthy of gestures meant only for lords and saints."

"Despite all my foolish words, I adore you, but I am a rude man, undeserving of your love. My offer is honorable. I swear the vows would be public and blessed by a priest from Tyndal, for I hold you in higher esteem than my own life." He waited.

Gytha lowered her eyes and said nothing.

"If you cannot otherwise bear the prospect of marriage to me, then think of my innocent child who loves you like the mother she never knew. Would you marry me for her sake?"

"Cruel man to have said that!"

"You saw how she missed you. Promise you will not abandon her again, whatever your answer to me."

"You would have me marry you for Sibely?" Her voice trembled.

He covered his eyes. "Nay, I truly cannot ask that you share my bed and life, a man whom you rightfully hate, even for my daughter. Refuse me with gentleness. I do beg for that mercy.

As for my child, I only ask that you visit again, as you have, for her sake. I shall stay away from you…"

"But why ask me to be your wife at all? We are not of equal rank…"

"Because I honor you above all other women," he whispered.

"Then I shall marry you, Crowner, despite your faults and rough ways."

He gasped and his eyes shone as if he had just seen a vision.

"But I have two conditions." She took his hand and put it against her cheek.

"I will swear anything!"

"Eat those berries and shave."

Chapter Thirty-five

"We are grateful for your protection and charity." Jacob ben Asser bowed to those gathered to see the family safely on the way to Norwich. From the fat, broad back of one of Tostig's more mature donkeys, Belia smiled. Little Baruch, soon to be formally granted the name, slept peacefully in his mother's arms as if the world held no harm for him.

Prioress Eleanor gazed at the impressive party of armed and mounted men who would protect this small group on the road. Ralf had gotten word to his brother, the sheriff, and Sir Fulke had dispatched the needed soldiers. "I grieve for all you suffered in our village," she said, turning her attention to Mistress Malka.

"If it had not been for your fine apothecary, my daughter would have died." Malka smiled at Sister Anne. "Instead she lives, and I have a grandson."

"And I, too, would be returning to Norwich, blinded by tears, had we not met Sister Anne here," Jacob added, then spoke again of his gratitude for the protection given his family, the kindness of the innkeeper and even his temporary jailer, as well as the diligence of Crowner Ralf in seeking justice.

Thus you teach us all the true meaning of forgiveness, the prioress said to herself, but she kept her thoughts private as they grew more uneasy. The violence against this family continued to anger her, but she had more cause to be troubled after Oseberne's death.

Although the murderer was dead, his body had been buried in sanctified ground. He had died untried for his crimes and never pronounced guilty of murder. As she well knew, some claimed that Oseberne had confessed any transgressions in the hearing of a priest and died a good Christian, forgiven all sins. A few others even whispered that what he had done had been no wickedness at all.

Eleanor shut her eyes to hide her musings. What she could not disguise was the flushing of outrage that painted her cheeks.

To her mind, the man had only bragged about the murders and thefts and never showed remorse. This was not her concept of a true confession, and she also suffered dissatisfaction with the lack of both trial and hanging. Opening her eyes and looking upward, she forced herself to remember that God must still judge the man's soul and would not be lax in due punishment where no repentance was felt. This time it was harder for her to feel comforted by this, but she was determined to be so.

Yet there had been a form of justice in the manner of his death. The bees, who had enjoyed the gentle care of Brother Gwydo, had wielded their special weapons against the man who had murdered their caretaker. In that, she found an odd contentment. Scripture did teach that vengeance must always belong to God, perhaps because mortals were too imperfect to judge without selfish motive. The bees had acted well on behalf of their Creator. She caught herself smiling.

But the moment of peace was brief. She suddenly felt light-headed standing in the hot summer air. Might she be sickening? Her head ached as if someone was pushing a hot metal rod into her temple. Eleanor took a deep breath. Most likely her courses were due, a condition that always make her uncomfortable in the heat.

She looked up at the sky. The sun was expanding with painful brightness, and the intensity of its power sucked strength from her. Her eyes began to hurt as well as her head. She longed to escape to the quiet of her cool and shaded chambers.

Determined not to let herself fall victim to self-indulgent weakness, Eleanor turned her attention again to the family of Jacob ben Asser. How relieved they must feel that they had only a few hours left of their journey back to the comfort of kindred and friends in Norwich.

Although their faith was not hers, they were of kind heart and gentle manner. If Jacob ben Asser and his family had been Christians, she would praise them for holding to their beliefs despite threatened slaughter. Indeed, most would condemn them for this obstinacy, but she confessed to God that she admired them anyway. In truth, it was a pity that they had not converted, but surely they would never forget Tyndal Priory. Perhaps one day…

With no warning, dizziness struck her hard. She staggered.

Sister Anne grasped her elbow, steadied her, and then asked with concern if all was well.

Forcing a bright smile, Eleanor denied illness, but her arm began to tingle as if needles were pricking it. A horse whinnied and she started. The sound hurt her head. Again, she stiffened her back, patted her friend's hand, and turned to matters other than this inconvenient frailty.

"Did not Mistress Malka promise to send you a precious manuscript on breathing difficulties for your collection," she murmured to the sub-infirmarian, "one written by a Jewish physician named Moshe ben Maimon?"

"This gift is in gratitude for saving her daughter and grandson. I told her that we had no need of thanks," Sister Anne replied, "but she insisted, saying that the work was a translation that my father, Benedict of Norwich, would have cherished."

Eleanor nodded. "Then we shall accept the offering with gratitude," she said, but the sound of her own voice was painfully loud and she fell silent.

Turning to look behind her, the prioress noticed that only Tostig and Signy, with her foster son by her side, had come from the village to see this family off. Gytha was tending the wounded Ralf, but they had sent their prayers for a safe journey. Was it shame that kept others away because they had unjustly accused

Jacob ben Asser of murdering Kenelm? Or was it due to hatred for the family that still festered in their hearts?

The reaction of the villagers to Oseberne's crimes of theft unsettled her. Because the victims had been Jewish, few cared that the baker robbed these innocent travelers to enrich himself. As for Kenelm, no one had liked the man. Some still regretted that a villager had been guilty, but no one grieved over the guard's murder. The only crime the village lamented was the murder of Brother Gwydo. Yet Gytha told her that some men believed he had betrayed his faith by slipping out of the priory to ask pardon of a Jew, and thus God had punished him.

She took a deep breath to calm herself, but the air seared her lungs like molten lead and the faint smell of her own sweat made her nauseous. Feeling lightheaded again, she shook her head, hoping to chase the dizziness away, and shut her eyes against the intense sunlight. When she opened them, she saw that the armed guard had surrounded the family, and the party was about to depart. As the prioress looked into the distance, the road to Norwich shimmered. Even the stones and trees glowed as if the sun had set them afire.

Just in time, Eleanor stopped herself from giving Jacob ben Asser and his family a blessing and instead wished them a safe journey, as did Prior Andrew and Brother Thomas. Sister Anne opened her arms and stepped forward to hug Mistress Malka, then kissed a finger and placed it against the cheek of the babe she had brought into the world. When the nun walked back to her side, Eleanor saw tears in her eyes and then noticed that the cheeks of Mistress Malka also glistened.

As the family slowly rode off, the mother and her babe on the donkey with the young father walking beside them, Eleanor saw extraordinary, shimmering circles of light begin to flow around each of their heads. The lights were unbearably bright, and her eyes watered with the pain. But she could not bear to look away and stared without blinking as if compelled by a force far greater than her own will.

With no warning, the prioress fell to her knees and pressed her hand against her heart.

Sister Anne knelt by her friend's side. "You are ill!" she whispered, frightened by the prioress' staring eyes and sudden pallor.

Eleanor grasped her friend's shoulder and pointed down the road. Her hand trembled. "The Holy Family," she murmured. "Do they not look like the Holy Family?"

◇◇◇

Years hence, the tale was told that the village of Tyndal had been honored to receive a visit from Saint Joseph and the Virgin Mary. There, in a stable, the wonder of the Bethlehem story had been recreated, an event intended to bring solace and reverent awe to the hearts of all who witnessed it.

But instead of humble joy, the villagers greeted the family with hate and violence, as the inhabitants of Sodom did God's angels. As a consequence, no one was allowed the privilege of seeing the miracle. Only the Prioress of Tyndal was found virtuous enough to receive the blessing of the vision, the story went, and so her reputation continued to grow as one especially favored by God.

Author's Notes

In England, Jewish immigration began with a warm invitation from William the Conqueror to the Jewish merchants of Rouen. His purpose was pragmatic. Skilled and well-connected businessmen were certainly good for an economy suffering the aftereffects of war. Christians were also barred from money-lending, although the need to borrow remained an economic necessity, and usury became the occupation quickly assigned to the Jewish community. The king then put these families under his protection and authority, thus allowing him to also profit handsomely from the relationship while protecting his "investments."

By the time of Edward I, however, English Jewry had been bled dry by exorbitant fees, taxes and other methods of paying for monarchial costs. (Despite Belia's observation about Henry III supporting Jewish plaintiffs in court against Christians, this king's record was very mixed.) But Edward had a new source to pay his debts, costs for building castles in Wales, and get money for those wars against the Scots. It was called the Italian financier.

Since the Jewish community no longer served his financial requirements, he may have concluded he could best use them for political gain by bowing to the barons' wish not to pay back loans they had previously begged. (Some of these had been needed by former de Montfort supporters to buy back the land taken from them by the king.) In any case, Edward launched a series of anti-Semitic proclamations that eventually led to the expulsion of the Jews from England in 1290. He was neither the first nor the last ruler to take this road, but it is a troubling asterisk next to the name of one so often praised as "the lawyer king."

The Statute of Jewry (*Statutum de Judeismo*) was signed by Edward I in late 1275. Although the need for borrowing continued and interest rates would always exist in some form, he concluded that usury by the Jewish community in particular had caused "divers evils and the disinheriting of good men." As of October 1275, no interest on old loans could accumulate, Edward would not lend his support to any repayment, and Jews were almost instantly prohibited from moneylending. In addition, large yellow badges became obligatory for all over the age of seven, a demand often imposed in the past but little enforced, and both men and women over the age of twelve were assessed yet another fine. Jews and Christians were also not allowed to live together (suggesting that they had been intermingling), and the Jewish communities were only allowed to reside in cities (*archa* towns) where the records of usurious debts had been kept.

To make up for this rather abrupt elimination of a major and obligatory profession, the statute encouraged the Jewish community to become merchants or even farmers, an odd suggestion for a group who had little opportunity in England to learn how to till the land. The permission to do business with Christian merchants and to "live by lawful trade and by their labour" sounds innocent enough until one discovers that movement, property transfers, and debt negotiations between merchants were severely restricted for the Jewish businessmen. The rules hardly made competition fair or equal, and just how does one run a farm without being able to stay around long enough to make sure the stewardship is honest?

For those interested in the provisions of the statute, a copy in readable English is easily obtained on the Internet. This is a far more complex subject than I can do justice to here, and the books by Richard Huscroft, Robin Mundill, and Cecil Roth, listed in my bibliography, are good places to start for those interested in a thorough discussion of Edward's rationale as well as the changing environment for the Jewish community.

It should be noted, however, that thirteenth-century England was not alone in this anti-Semitic trend. When I tried to decide where Jacob and his family might go, I found few places in Europe where massacres had not recently occurred or banishments were not forthcoming.

Anti-Semitism was widespread and often virulent in the medieval era, but the conclusion that all medieval Christians hated or shunned all Jews is not an accurate assumption. There have always been some who do not join the mobs. Those Germans who saved Jewish friends and even strangers during the Holocaust are an example. More frequently, many cast aside common prejudice when it was practical or lucrative to do so.

Jewish doctors treated Christian patients. The reverse was also true. Contrary to some secular laws and much Church opposition, Christians worked as servants for Jewish families. Merchants, no matter what their religion, cooperated when it was mutually beneficial. Children of both faiths often played together, a fact that makes the bizarre stories concocted about the deaths of boys like William of Norwich all the more tragic.

Despite the prohibitions against Jewish merchants belonging to guilds, Benedict fil Abraham was welcomed into one in 1268 by Simon le Draper, Mayor of Winchester. This may have been encouraged by King Henry III, who had a financial interest, and was certainly contentious and a unique situation. However, Robert Burton's statement in his 1621 *Anatomy of Melancholy* remains true: "No rule is so general, which admits not some exception."

No matter what the era, people rationalize their actions, noble or ignoble, with reference to faith or other ethical codes. (In the United States, we both defended and excoriated slavery with biblical quotes.) To say that Christians in the medieval period never did the same is to disregard an ancient human custom. So Oseberne justifies his hatred of Jacob ben Asser by quoting the teaching of a priest, while Prioress Eleanor and Brother

Thomas opt for compassion in a similar fashion. We may find their language, imagery, and reasoning tortuous or alien, but, were their discussions put into modern dialogue, we would find much the same points of view reported in the morning news.

The story told by Brother Thomas about Bernard of Clairvaux is based on the abbot's letter in 1146, promoting the second crusade, in which he also denounced violence against the Jewish communities and warned against following extremists like Peter the Hermit, a man who led many innocents to their deaths while carefully saving his own life. Pope Gregory X, who reigned from 1271 to 1276, did write a letter in 1272 condemning forced baptisms, aggression against the Jews, and the fabrications of blood libel, although he himself had been on crusade with Edward I and was hardly the medieval version of the latte liberal.

Neither of these men extended his remarks to include compassion toward Muslims, that being an era of war between the two faiths, but many ordinary crusaders did remain in the land where they had gone to fight those deemed infidels, married local women, and occasionally converted to Islam.

Like Prioress Eleanor, most medieval Christians hoped for conversions, an attitude common to any proselytizing creed, but it would have taken a fossilized heart not to react in horror at violence perpetrated on peaceful men and mothers with their babes in arms.

Jewish divorce in the Middle Ages was somewhat easier than Christian marriage dissolution, but it was still rare and looked upon with extreme disfavor within the community. One of the reasons for divorce was a childless marriage after ten years, but, if the wife refused consent, honored rabbinical opinion said that the dissolution should be prohibited. It wasn't always, but familial rather than political concern was the ruling factor.

A short note for those who might not have recognized the name: Moshe ben Maimon is possibly better known as Moses Maimonides. Sister Anne would have treasured any of his medical works.

◇◇◇

Lay brothers in a religious house were men who had taken the vows of the order but were not ordained and were primarily employed in manual labor. (Lay sisters performed a similar function.) They usually had little education and were of a lower social class. In many cases, their dress was slightly different to distinguish them from the choir monks. Choir monks were supposed to spend most of their time in study, prayer, and singing the office. Their education was expected to include knowledge of Latin. And so Adelard might well be miffed when told he could only enter Tyndal Priory as a lay brother, since he had expected to become a higher ranked choir monk. If his vocation were more his father's wish than his own, he may soon decide that running a profitable business was a more congenial choice.

Bees are striking in appearance and have long fascinated me. At age four, I was stung trying to pet one. Many decades later, I keep a more respectful distance, but I still love to watch a great bumble rolling in a native poppy and am amazed at the organization of honeybees, a society that includes guards and undertakers as well as workers and leaders.

In the Middle Ages, bees were not accurately "sexed." That was not done until centuries later. In 1609, Charles Butler wrote *The Feminine Monarchie* in which he established that queens ruled the hive, not kings. From at least the time of the Greeks through the sixteenth century, it was assumed that the queen was a king and the mating ritual a battle, after which the bee troops settled down to making honey for human consumption and the best wax for our candles. The troops mentioned by Brother Gwydo are male drones, eager to mate with the queen who flies through the swarm. Sadly, the drones die after mating. The "tooting" mentioned by Brother Gwydo is actually a sound emitted by queens which can be heard several yards away.

Today, bees continue to suffer from diseases and seasonal death, but our methods of collecting honey no longer require killing off the weaker hives with sulphur fumes. Nontoxic smoke is still used to calm them during honey harvesting, but modern beekeepers are interested in preserving as many bee lives as possible.

The average honeybee is not normally aggressive, but the hives that Oseberne knocked over had been harassed before. These bees had learned to attack when someone rushed at them and committed violence against their home, as some boys in this story had done previously. In Oseberne's case, he was fatally allergic to the sting, and there was no remedy to save his life in the thirteenth century. Others might have suffered much pain, but the stinging would not have killed them. Each honeybee, however, dies after stinging once.

As a final note, there was good news recently from England. The native black honeybee of Brother Gwydo's time, almost destroyed by a virus 100 years ago, is coming back. Unlike the yellow-striped variety, familiar to many of us, the black honeybee is darker, bigger, and protected by thicker, longer hair, which makes it a hardier species in the northern climates.

Bibliography

The following list includes only a sample of books available on Jewish history in late thirteenth-century England. Since it is a subject to which I shall return, as King Edward continues down the slope to the 1290 expulsion, more will be included in future mysteries.

For details on beekeeping, I am grateful to Earl Flewellen, of E. G. Flewellen's Bee Farm in Port Costa, California, who took time from his bees to answer my clueless questions, lend me books on the subject, and introduce me to his incredible organic honey.

As always, I am indebted to scholars who pull fascinating details out of the past, study them, and share the results with those of us eager to learn.

When I make a mistake in any fact, it is solely *mea culpa*.

The ABC and XYZ of Bee Culture (41st Edition), by Amos Ives Root, A.I. Root Company, 2006.

Expulsion: England's Jewish Solution, by Richard Huscroft, Tempus Publishing, 2006.

A History of Jewish Gynaecological Texts in the Middle Ages, by Ron Barkai, Brill, 1998.

A History of the Jews in England (3rd Edition), by Cecil Roth, Oxford University Press, 1964.

Jewish Women in Europe in the Middle Ages: A Quiet Revolution, by Simha Goldin, Manchester University Press, 2011.

Licoricia of Winchester: Marriage, Motherhood and Murder in the Medieval Anglo-Jewish Community, by Suzanne Bartlet (ed. Patricia Skinner), Vallentine Mitchell, 2009.

England's Jewish Solution: Experiment and Expulsion, 1262–1290, by Robin R. Mundill, Cambridge University Press, 1998.

The Trotula: An English Translation of the Medieval Compendium of Women's Medicine, edited and translated by Monica H. Green, University of Pennsylvania Press, 2002.

World History of Beekeeping and Honey Hunting, by Eva Crane, Routledge, 1999.

To receive a free catalog of Poisoned Pen Press titles, please contact us in one of the following ways:

Phone: 1-800-421-3976
Facsimile: 1-480-949-1707
Email: info@poisonedpenpress.com
Website: www.poisonedpenpress.com

Poisoned Pen Press
6962 E. First Ave. Ste 103
Scottsdale, AZ 85251